## To Scotland and Love

Tara ran up the last steps and opened the Tower door.

Then, as she pushed it open, she heard Talbot cry "Help!" and moved swiftly out into the sunshine.

Just in front of her, Talbot's cousin had his back to her.

She knew he intended to stab Talbot.

Then, as if somebody was telling her what to do, she raised her arm.

With all her strength, she threw the dirk she had taken off the wall at the assassin's back. . . .

### *A Camfield Novel of Love by Barbara Cartland*

*"Barbara Cartland's novels are all distinguished by their intelligence, good sense, and good nature. . . ."*

—ROMANTIC TIMES

*"Who could give better advice on how to keep your romance going strong than the world's most famous romance novelist, Barbara Cartland?"*

—THE STAR

Camfield Place,
Hatfield
Hertfordshire,
England

Dearest Reader,

Camfield Novels of Love mark a very exciting era of my books with Jove. They have already published nearly two hundred of my titles since they became my first publisher in America, and now all my original paperback romances in the future will be published exclusively by them.

As you already know, Camfield Place in Hertfordshire is my home, which originally existed in 1275, but was rebuilt in 1867 by the grandfather of Beatrix Potter.

It was here in this lovely house, with the best view in the county, that she wrote *The Tale of Peter Rabbit*. Mr. McGregor's garden is exactly as she described it. The door in the wall that the fat little rabbit could not squeeze underneath and the goldfish pool where the white cat sat twitching its tail are still there.

I had Camfield Place blessed when I came here in 1950 and was so happy with my husband until he died, and now with my children and grandchildren, that I know the atmosphere is filled with love and we have all been very lucky.

It is easy here to write of love and I know you will enjoy the Camfield Novels of Love. Their plots are definitely exciting and the covers very romantic. They come to you, like all my books, with love.

Bless you,

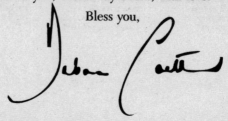

# CAMFIELD NOVELS OF LOVE

### by Barbara Cartland

A NEW CAMFIELD NOVEL OF LOVE BY

# BARBARA CARTLAND

## To Scotland and Love

JOVE BOOKS, NEW YORK

# TO SCOTLAND AND LOVE

A Jove Book / published by arrangement with
the author

PRINTING HISTORY
Jove edition / September 1993

ISBN: 0-515-11197-X

Jove Books are published by The Berkley Publishing Group,
200 Madison Avenue, New York, New York 10016.
The name "JOVE" and the "J" logo
are trademarks belonging to Jove Publications, Inc.

PRINTED IN THE UNITED STATES OF AMERICA

10  9  8  7  6  5  4  3  2  1

# Author's Note

WHEREVER the Scots go, they take with them their tartans, their whisky—which can be made only in Scotland—the Haggis, and the Reels.

Reels were known throughout Scotland in the sixteenth century, but during the seventeenth the Presbyterian Church severely discouraged social dancing.

By 1700, the Reel seems to have survived, but only in the Highlands, where the Presbyterian influence was the weakest.

After 1700, when the Church became more tolerant of dancing, Reels reappeared in the Scottish Lowlands.

At about 1770, the only specific Reel mentioned in Scottish literature is *The Threesome*.

Seventy years later this was widely superseded by *The Foursome Reel*.

Reels in a similar form did occur in England and Wales, while a different kind was known in Ireland.

*The Eightsome Reel*, which is included in country dancing throughout the United Kingdom, does not conform to the earlier Reels.

Composed in about 1870, it incorporates the figures of a Reel dating from about 1818.

The Haggis is entirely and completely a part of Scotland and now the Scots have introduced it all over the world.

A real Haggis is made of sheep's pluck (lungs, heart, and liver) which is boiled with beef fat for three hours.

It is then minced with oatmeal, onions, and seasoning and a large Haggis is sewn into a sheep's stomach.

The Haggis is always the most important dish at a Burns Supper that is steeped in tradition.

It begins with the *Selkirk Grace* which Robert Burns first used in 1793 at a dinner given by the Earl of Selkirk.

Then to the cry of "Hail Great Chieftain o' the Puddin-race!" and the skirl of the bagpipes, the Haggis is carried in.

The Chairman reads the Burns address, *To a Haggis,* during which a dirk is plunged through the skin of the Haggis.

The proof of a successful Burns Supper is the intensity of the singing, the poetry reading, and the quality of the main tribute of the evening, known as *The Immortal Memory.*

To Scotland and Love

## chapter one

# 1880

TALBOT Marsham looked round Whites Club.

He was saying good-bye not only to the Club, but also to its members, many of whom were his friends.

He had always enjoyed going there, knowing that he would find half a dozen people with whom he had been at School.

There were also those with whom he had become friendly either at University or later in life.

But the Club which meant so much to him and to many of his contemporaries was becoming expensive.

He knew he could not afford the membership fee for the coming year.

'I shall miss it,' he thought.

A friend came up and offered him a drink, which he accepted gratefully.

He knew he could not buy himself one.

If he did he would have to go hungry to-night

and, as he was well aware, his rent was overdue.

He sat down in one of the comfortable leather armchairs.

As he did so, he asked himself how things could have got so bad.

"You are looking depressed, Talbot," his friend Henry Johnson remarked. "What is the matter?"

"Need you ask?" Talbot replied. "There is nothing new since I last saw you."

"You mean you are 'down on your uppers' again?" Henry asked. "Have a glass of Champagne and cheer up. I am sure we can find an answer to your problem."

"God knows what it can be," Talbot replied.

Henry had been with him at Eton.

Although he was not rich himself, his Father was well off and he did not lack anything he required.

"I can let you have a 'tenner,' " Henry offered.

"I would be grateful for half that," Talbot answered. "But to be serious, Henry, this cannot go on."

"Then you have been unable to find employment of any sort?"

"I tried three different places yesterday," Talbot replied, "but you know as well as I do that the last thing they need are Gentlemen who have no qualifications apart from a Public School education."

"That is true," Henry said. "I am sure if I had to work I would not know where to begin!"

Both men were aware there were very few Gentlemen since the Industrial Revolution who had gone into Industry.

It was frowned on by their contemporaries, and Industry itself did not want them.

In Social circles they talked scornfully of a man who was "in the City."

This was despite the fact that for the first time in history the Prince of Wales patronised the Jewish Financiers and made them his friends.

The majority of the aristocrats, however, thought it degrading to work.

Their sons were well off, so they had nothing to do but attend Race-Meetings, watch Polo, and gamble at the Clubs in St. James's Street.

This, in some cases, had proved disastrous, especially when the gamblers owned property.

Whole streets and Squares changed hands over the card table.

More than one young man had retired to the country when his pockets were empty and his Father would no longer meet his gambling debts.

"The difficulty is," Talbot said reflectively, "that while Eton and Oxford educated us—I think extremely well—the knowledge we have is not saleable in the world as it is to-day."

"I suppose it would have been more sensible if we had gone into a Regiment," Henry said. "We did discuss it, if you remember, but your Father was against you going into a Scottish Regiment, and your Mother could not think of you being in an English one."

This was true, and it was another complication in Talbot's life.

His Mother had been Lady Janet McCairn, daughter of the Earl of Cairnloch.

He was Chieftain of the Clan and lived in the North of Scotland.

The Earl had what amounted to an obsessive hatred of the English.

Therefore, when his eldest daughter wanted to marry a Sassenach, he refused to contemplate such a *mésalliance*.

"If ye marry this damned Englishman after the way the English have treated the Scots, then I will have nothing more to do with you, and will not acknowledge you as my daughter!"

These were strong words, spoken with the authority which the Earl exerted over his Clan.

He never for a moment thought that his daughter would defy him.

But Lady Janet had fallen in love.

\* \* \*

Among the guests who had come to shoot grouse with one of their friends was Frederick Marsham.

He was the son of a well-known Statesman and considered an exceptional *parti* by those who had *débutante* daughters.

They had been paraded before him ever since he had left School.

At twenty-seven, however, he was still a bachelor simply because he had never fallen in love.

From the moment he set eyes on Lady Janet he lost his heart.

She, according to her family, lost her head.

The Earl had always been determined that a Sassenach should never cross the threshold of his Castle.

When his daughter wished to marry one, it made her a leper as far as he was concerned.

The only thing that Lady Janet and Frederick Marsham could do was to elope.

He had not carried her off at midnight in romantic fashion.

He had called on the Earl and told him he wished to marry his daughter.

The Earl had raged at him with a fury which would have struck one of the McCairn Clansmen like lightning.

The victim would certainly have collapsed under the force of it.

Frederick Marsham merely treated the man he wished to make his Father-in-law with a quiet contempt.

This made the Earl more furious than he was already.

"Surely, My Lord," he argued, "you must be aware that your hatred of the English is completely out of date. I admit that the Duke of Cumberland behaved abominably when he invaded Scotland. I admit the Clearances, which were attributed to English influence, caused a great deal of suffering to many of your people, but all that is in the past and you cannot now continue to loathe a country with which yours is united."

That was exactly what the Earl did feel.

He told Frederick Marsham that if he did not

leave his Castle immediately, he would have him thrown out by the servants.

Frederick Marsham behaved with dignity.

He asked the Earl to reconsider his decision.

When the Earl replied only that he would curse him from now until his dying day he accepted the inevitable.

"I think, My Lord," he said, "it is something you will regret. I bid you good-day and accept your decision never to enter your house again."

He walked from the Chieftain's Room and down the stairs.

Waiting for him in the Hall was Lady Janet.

She had known only too well what would be the outcome of the interview between her Father and the man she loved.

But Frederick had insisted that he should behave correctly so that he could not reproach himself in the future.

Now, as he came down the stairs, Janet looked up at him.

She knew by the expression on his face that, as she had anticipated, her Father had refused to listen to anything Frederick had to say.

Frederick put out his hand, and she slipped hers into it.

He stopped still, looked at her lovely face turned to his, and said:

"You are quite certain, my Darling, that you are prepared to come with me? I think it is unlikely that your Father will ever forgive you if you do."

Lady Janet sighed.

"You know I cannot stay here without you," she replied, "and unless we can be together, I have no . . . wish to go on . . . living."

The way she spoke was simple and not in any way dramatic.

Frederick knew that what she said came from her heart.

He raised her hand and kissed it.

"So be it," he said.

His carriage was waiting outside and Lady Janet's trunks were in the Hall.

It took a little time before they could be strapped onto the carriage, but there was no sign of the Earl.

As they drove away from the Castle, Lady Janet did not look back.

Frederick's arms were round her, and he kissed her until the drive was left behind.

Then there was only the wild moorland around them.

Contrary to the expectation of the McCairn family, the marriage was blissfully happy.

Lady Janet produced a son, which was everything that Frederick Marsham wanted.

Unfortunately she had no more children, but they were content.

Frederick did not object when she had wanted to call her son Talbot.

It was one of the family names which was ingrained in the history of Scotland.

There was never a word from the Earl or from any of the McCairn relations.

The only person who knew that Lady Janet missed her own kith and kin and Scotland itself was her son, Talbot.

When he was young she had related the legends of the Highlands to him.

She had stirred his imagination with stories of the Scottish heroes who had been part of her own childhood.

Talbot, when he was older, realised, when she talked of her homeland, that there was a wistfulness in her voice.

He knew that however happy she was in England, one part of her heart would always belong to the land where she was born.

She was, however, very careful not to let her husband think she was anything but extremely happy, which, in fact, she was.

When Frederick died three years ago, she had longed only to join him.

She believed that they would be together in Heaven as they had been on earth.

It was after Frederick Marsham's death that things became difficult.

His Father had always been a rich man, but he had in his old age made an unfortunate number of investments which had swallowed up his capital.

His son inherited little but debts.

Frederick had expected to own a comfortable Estate in the Country and to be able to live as his ancestors had.

But he found, when his Father was dead, that the Estate, which was in bad repair, had to be sold.

The proceeds from the house and its contents only just covered the outstanding debts.

What was worse was that Frederick himself had no income except what he received from his Father.

He struggled, rather late in life, to find some other source of income, but failed.

Fortunately, his son, Talbot, had already been educated at the best and most expensive School in England.

He had enjoyed his time at Oxford enormously and had made a great number of friends.

It had never occurred to Talbot to worry as to how his fees were paid.

He had never denied himself the clothes, books, or horses he particularly desired.

His Father had been subjected to a bombshell when he had found himself penniless.

To Talbot, on his death, it was an unbelievable catastrophe.

"What are we going to live on, Mama?" he asked his Mother.

"I have no idea, Darling," she replied. "Your Father always looked after everything. I never asked questions about where the money came from."

Talbot discovered that in the two years before his Father's death, Frederick Marsham had used up every penny of the sale.

He had also incurred an overdraft which had to be met.

The only fortunate thing was that Lady Janet possessed some very fine jewellery.

It had been given her by her adoring husband

from the first moment they had run away together.

Talbot took charge, knowing his Mother did not understand in any way what should be done.

He sold her jewellery very carefully, piece by piece.

He also reduced their standard of living by employing two servants when they had previously had six.

The jewellery had gradually dwindled away.

Finally, Lady Janet had her wish and joined her husband in Heaven.

Talbot was grateful that he did not at first have to sell the London house in which they lived, because it would have upset his Mother to do so.

Once again, however, there were debts.

The area where the house was situated was not fashionable at this particular moment.

He sold it for a small sum and moved into lodgings.

For the first time in his life, at the age of twenty-five, he knew he had to try to find work.

It was, he discovered, almost impossible for a Gentleman.

When he mentioned what he was looking for in Whites, his friends stared at him as if they could not believe what they were hearing.

"Good Heavens, Talbot!" one of them exclaimed, "you cannot really spend your life in some fusty office, or travel to the City like those common chaps in bowler hats."

"It is what I have to do," Talbot said quietly,

"unless I am to end up working as a crossing-sweeper."

They laughed at this as if it were a great joke.

But to Talbot it was a nightmare from which he could not awake.

When his house was sold he had moved into a bachelor flat in Half Moon Street.

It was an attractive one which had been used by the Bucks and Beaux during the Regency.

He started on the First Floor which was the most expensive.

He had been forced to move steadily upwards, until now he was in the attic.

It was considered unsuitable for a lodger.

Only because the Landlord was fond of Talbot was he permitted to use it for a few shillings a week.

"You'll be hot in t'Summer an' cold in t'Winter," he said. "It's not a proper place for a Gentleman."

"It will do for a Gentleman with no money," Talbot replied, "so I would be very grateful if you could let me have it, as I cannot afford anything better."

"You've allus bin a reliable tenant, Mister Marsham," the Landlord said, "an' I'd be sorry to lose yer. Take the attic if ye want it, but don't blame me if yer find it's worse than a bed o' nails!"

"I will not do that," Talbot replied, "and thank you very much. I am most grateful."

He moved all his possessions up into the attic.

He was aware, however, that even this would prove too expensive unless he could find work.

"There must be something I can do!" he said to Henry.

"I suppose you could be a coachman or a groom," Henry replied, "but I cannot see you eating in the Servants' Hall."

"Do you think one of these millionaire friends of the Prince of Wales would take me on their staff?" Talbot asked.

Henry said, "The answer is probably No."

Talbot knew this was true.

It did not, however, make it any easier to find something to do for which he would be paid.

He knew that Henry would help him if he could.

He would doubtless pay for him to remain a member of Whites.

But he had a pride which was unquenchable, and which doubtless came from his Scottish blood.

It made him determined to take as little as possible from Henry.

He was aware that if he accepted the ten pounds Henry offered him, it would have to be spent on the rent.

The meagre meals he consumed, when he did not have an invitation to a luncheon or a dinner, would take up the rest.

He was fortunate in that his Grandfather had been so well-known in political circles.

His Mother had a title.

He was therefore on the guest list of all the great hostesses of London.

Talbot was assured of a dinner or supper almost every night in one or other of the great houses.

During the Season he also had a number of invitations to luncheon.

Inevitably, there were days when he had to eat very frugally in Shepherd Market.

Alternatively, he could go to Whites in the hope that one of the members would pay for his meal.

He resented bitterly not being able to reciprocate their hospitality with invitations of his own.

He refused a great number of drinks he was offered.

Simply because he knew he could not pay for a round when it came to his turn.

"What am I to do, Henry?" he asked, now in despair.

"I honestly do not know," Henry answered. "I told my Father of your plight, but he merely gave me a long lecture on what a mistake it was to run into debt."

He gave a somewhat humourless laugh before he added:

"The bill had just come in for those last horses I bought and the Chaise which I ordered from the Coach Builders."

"I thought that was an extravagance," Talbot said. "After all, the one you were driving before was perfectly adequate."

"But not really up-to-date," Henry said. "I cannot see why I should pinch and scrape when Papa is rolling in money."

"Mind, you are certain of that!" Talbot said warningly. "You must know, as I do, that there has been what amounts to a crisis on the Stock Exchange."

Henry shrugged his shoulders.

"I never read the Financial Columns of the newspapers," he said. "My Father has the best people to advise him, and he does not need mine."

Talbot thought it was the same attitude he had himself taken up where his Father was concerned.

It had landed him in the gutter, with no means of getting out of it.

He was only thankful that his Mother had not had to live as he did.

He knew how much she would have disliked it.

"I will not give in," he told himself. "I will find something to do if it kills me!"

He allowed Henry to give him luncheon.

He then walked back to his lodgings.

He had nothing to do before this evening when he had accepted an invitation to dine with the Countess of Warwick.

The food there would be superlative, and so would the drink.

He thought, with a faint sense of humour, that if only he was a camel, he could eat enough to last him to the end of the week.

He reached his lodgings at Number 24, Half Moon Street.

The Porter opened the door to him.

"Ow, there ye be, Mr. Marsham!" he exclaimed. "There's a Gen'man askin' fer ye."

"A Gentleman?" Talbot exclaimed. "Who is it? Did he give you his name?"

"Nah," the Porter replied, "but 'e says as 'e were

14

very anxious to 'ave a word wi' ye, so Oi takes 'im upstairs, knowin' ye'd be in sooner or later."

"I wonder who it can be?" Talbot said.

He never encouraged any of his friends, with the exception of Henry, to visit him in Half Moon Street.

He knew they would be shocked at the attic in which he was living.

They would perhaps make a joke about it, which he would find embarrassing.

" 'E be upstairs, Mr. Marsham," the Porter said. "A Scottish Gen'man Oi thinks 'e be—from th' way 'e talks."

Talbot stared at the Porter, and was about to ask a question.

Then he thought the best thing he could do was to go and find out for himself.

He climbed the stairs to the attic.

He thought that few men of his acquaintance would enjoy the last flight of stairs, which were very steep.

Turning the handle, he opened the door, bending his head.

The doorway was only a little over five feet from the ground, and he was a tall man.

The ceiling slanted in on both sides of the room.

There were several stalwart wooden posts to hold it up.

The only redeeming feature was the window at the North end.

Many years ago it had been enlarged for an Artist who had chosen to live there.

It had an excellent north light, which he had required for his painting.

It certainly made the attic more cheerful than it would otherwise have been.

From the window there was a fine view of the roofs of Mayfair, and in particular, of Shepherd Market.

Sitting in an upright chair near the window was an elderly man whom Talbot had never seen before.

He was wearing a plaid cloak which seemed strange and out of date in London.

Although he was bare-headed, he was holding in his hand what appeared to Talbot to be a tam-o'-shanter.

As Talbot entered, the man rose to his feet.

"Ah think," he said with a strong Scottish accent, "ye'll be Mr. Talbot Marsham?"

"That is correct," Talbot replied, "and I am curious to know why you have called on me."

"Ah came t' London," the Scotsman answered, "tae look for your Mother, the Lady Janet."

"I know you will be sorry to learn that my Mother is dead," Talbot replied, "and as I am sure you have come from Scotland, will you tell me your name?"

"It is Andrew McCairn," the Scotsman replied.

"Then you are one of the Clan to which my Mother belonged."

"That is indeed true," Andrew McCairn replied. "And 'tis bad news, verry bad news that Her Ladyship's no longer alive. We were not aware of that in Scotland."

"It was three years ago," Talbot said, "but I naturally did not notify her Father, the Earl, because he has never communicated with her since she married my Father."

"I knew that, Mr. Marsham," Andrew McCairn said. "But the Earl of Cairnloch, who was your Grandfather, died two months ago and we, the Elders, hae been trying ever since tae find your Mother."

It suddenly occurred to Talbot that perhaps, although it seemed extremely unlikely, the Earl had left his Mother some money.

In which case, it would certainly be a godsend if it was now his.

"You say my Grandfather died two months ago," he said aloud. "He must have been very old?"

"Aye, nigh on eighty-five, but a fine man for all that! He was deeply respected by the Clan."

"My Mother often spoke of him," Talbot said, "and I suppose her only brother, who was a few years younger than her, must now be your Chieftain."

"Lord Donald died many years ago," Andrew replied. "He was never verry strong and he was only sixteen when he succumbed during one very cold winter."

"My Mother was not aware of that," Talbot said. "As you know, she had no communication with her family."

"That is why I had a hard job finding ye," Andrew answered. "They told me at the house where Her Ladyship once lived that you were here."

"Then I am afraid, although it is very kind of you to come so far," Talbot said, "that your journey has been in vain."

He looked round the small attic a little helplessly before he said:

"I feel I should offer you some refreshment, but unfortunately I have nothing up here at the moment."

"Nae, nae," Andrew said quickly. "Ah've eaten a good meal, and Ah have no need of anything mair than tae talk to ye aboot the future."

"The future?" Talbot questioned.

"Ah came South to England to find Her Ladyship," Andrew explained, "and to tell her that as her Faither the Earl is dead, that she was the Chieftain of the Clan."

Talbot looked at him in surprise.

"I had forgotten until you said that," Talbot exclaimed, "that my Mother told me that in Scotland the inheritance can go through the female line if there is no male heir. But, of course, she would have assumed, once her Father died, that her brother would become the next Chieftain."

"The place," Andrew said solemnly, "would hae been filled by Lady Janet, but noo that she's no longer with us, it is, of course, Mr. Marsham, yours!"

Talbot stared at him.

He could not for a moment believe what he had heard.

"Mine?" he said after a long silence. "But how can I be your Chieftain?"

**18**

"Ye are now," Andrew McCairn said solemnly, "the Earl of Cairnloch. And Ah'm begging ye on behalf of the Elders of the Clan to return with me tae Scotland and take up the place that has been left vacant by your Grandfather's death."

He spoke as if he were proclaiming from a pulpit.

Talbot was stunned.

Never in his wildest dreams had he thought there was any chance of him going to Scotland.

He had never imagined for one moment that his Mother would be called back to be the Chieftain of the Clan.

Yet he could understand that, as she was dead and could not become the Countess of Cairnloch, the title and the Chieftainship would go to him.

It was such a shock that, hardly knowing what he was doing, he rose to his feet.

He walked to the window, to stand looking out with unseeing eyes over the roofs.

The sun was shining, and it seemed to him that everything glimmered and glistened.

He felt as if he had been suddenly wafted from the darkness of despair into a light that came from Heaven.

He could almost believe that his Mother was looking down at him and telling him that it was just what she wanted for him.

She wanted him to look after the people to whom she belonged.

Andrew McCairn did not speak.

His eyes were on Talbot's back.

What he had seen of the young man so far pleased him.

He was tall, good-looking, and broad-shouldered.

There was something frank and straight-forward about him which Andrew had liked from the first moment he came into the attic.

After some time Talbot turned back.

"Are you really saying," he asked in a low voice, "that you want me in Scotland? You are sure there is nobody else the Clan would rather have?"

"Ye are the rightful heir," Andrew said, "and the Cairns who are old enough hae never forgotten your Mother."

Talbot longed to reply that the Scots never forgot anything.

That included his Grandfather's animosity towards his Father.

It had made him never forgive his daughter for marrying a Sassenach.

Aloud he said:

"I could come back with you—in fact I would like to do so—but I want to make sure that I am accepted by your people."

"They are *your* people, My Lord," Andrew corrected him.

Talbot drew in his breath at the way Andrew addressed him.

"Am I really the Earl of Cairnloch?" he asked. "I find it hard to believe!"

"It be your right, according to Scottish law," Andrew assured him, "and the Elders will accept you, although I should tell you there be another applicant."

"Who is that?" Talbot asked.

"Perhaps your Mother told you that she had a sister?"

"Yes, of course," Talbot replied. "My Mother often spoke of her. She was, however, very hurt that her sister Heather never wrote to her from the time she left the Castle."

"She would have obeyed her Faither's orders," Andrew said. "In fact, he issued instructions tae everybody that Lady Janet was nae longer his daughter and should not be spoken of by anybody who called himself a McCairn."

"I think that is what my Mother expected him to do," Talbot answered, "and I think in such circumstances, it was very brave of her to run away with the man she loved."

He spoke somewhat aggressively, as if he thought Andrew would contradict him.

But the old man merely said:

"Feelings against the English run very deep in Scotland, and your Grandfaither was a man who neverr forgave anyone who disobeyed him."

"Feelings against the English!" Talbot responded. "Then do you seriously believe they will accept me? And who is the other applicant?"

"That is what I was just about tae tell ye," Andrew replied. "It is the son of Lady Heather. She married a Cousin, a McCairn. The son is now aged twenty. His name is Alastair."

"And the McCairns would not rather have my Cousin Alastair than me?" Talbot asked.

Andrew shook his head.

"It is you who are the rightful heir, and the McCairns want things done in the traditional way. As your Mother is noo with God, Ah know I am right in taking ye back as our Chieftain."

Talbot drew in his breath. Then he said:

"Very well, Andrew. I shall be very glad to go with you. But you will understand that I have various friends I must see before I leave, and perhaps I should also point out that I do not possess a kilt!"

Andrew laughed.

"That can be easily remedied, M'Lorrd, an' Ah will of course await your convenience. After all, it's already taken me two weeks since Ah reached London tae find out where your Mother lived, and to meet ye."

"Very well," Talbot agreed. "We will go in three or four days' time. However, I think I should tell you that I have no money with which to pay my expenses on the journey."

"Ah have all the money needed," Andrew said. "And as the Earl, you're a verry rich man. Ah'll advance ye anything you require."

Talbot stared at him.

"Do you mean that?"

"Ah have an acoont at the Bank o' Scotland," Andrew explained. "Ah can cash a cheque there for any sum Your Lordship cares tae mention."

Talbot put his hand up to his forehead.

He wondered if he was dreaming, and if he would suddenly wake up.

If he did, he would find himself in the small, rather uncomfortable bed tucked away in a corner of the attic.

As if Andrew followed the way he was thinking, he said:

"Ah admit Ah'm surprised, My Lord, tae find ye awa' up here in the clouds if there's no reason for it. But perrhaps ye have a reason and you're an Artist?"

It flashed through Talbot's mind that it would not auger well for the Clan if Andrew was to say he was sleeping in a garret because he could not afford anything better.

It also cast aspersions upon his Father, who had carried off his Mother from the comfort and importance of a Castle.

With an effort he forced a smile to his lips.

"I am not surprised," he replied, "that you thought I might be an Artist, and in fact an Artist lodged here before me. But my reason is rather different."

He saw that Andrew was listening and went on:

"I am in fact writing a book, and I wanted somewhere where it was quiet and, you might almost say, amongst the clouds. I found, because I could look over the roofs and up at the sky, that this place was inspiring, while it was difficult to write in more formal surroundings."

"Ah've always understood, My Lord," Andrew replied, "that Authors, like Artists, must hae the proper background when they are worrking."

"You are right," Talbot said, "and I hope when finally my book is published that you will read and enjoy it."

"Ah shall be verry proud tae do so," Andrew said quietly.

Feeling a little guilty, Talbot said quickly:

"I would ask you to dinner with me, but tonight I have promised to dine with the Countess of Warwick, and you will understand that it would upset Her Ladyship's numbers if I were unable to turn up."

"Ah understand, My Lord," Andrew said. "And you must no' worry aboot me. Ah believe Ah know of a Scottish Tailor in London an' to-morrow we will go therre and see if he can provide ye with a kilt. It is somethin' Ah think ye should hae before ye arrive in the North."

"Thank you. That would be very helpful," Talbot said.

He escorted the old man downstairs, feeling embarrassed because he had difficulty descending the very steep steps from the attic floor.

There was no carriage waiting for the Scotsman.

He assured Talbot, however, that he could find his way to Albermarle Street, where he was staying in a quiet Hotel.

"Do not trouble to come to me to-morrow morning," Talbot said. "I will arrive at your Hotel at ten o'clock, if that is not too early?"

Andrew chuckled.

"In Scotland we rise with the sun," he said, "and sleep when it goes doon."

"Thank you for coming. Thank you very much for finding me," Talbot said as he shook him by the hand. "I will try to be ready to leave with you on Friday morning. Will we be travelling by train?"

Andrew shook his head.

" 'Tis easier by ship," he said.

"Very well," Talbot replied. "I will leave you to make the bookings."

"Ah will do that, M'Lorrd, and Ah'm thanking God that Ah have found ye and now the Clan will nae longer be without a Chieftain."

He walked briskly away down Half Moon Street towards Piccadilly.

Talbot watched him for some minutes.

He could hardly believe what he had just heard.

He knew his whole world had turned upside-down and the future was no longer frightening, but golden.

At the same time, it was a life of which he knew nothing, except from his Mother.

He would be like a small boy going to School for the first time.

He put his hand up to his forehead.

'I must have somebody to help me,' he thought, 'otherwise I shall make a series of mistakes and perhaps be the laughing stock of the Clan.'

It was a sensible idea, but the question was—who could assist him?

## *chapter two*

JUST as he was going through the door of his lodgings, Talbot remembered his Mother's friend, General Sir Iain MacDowall.

He had not seen him for nearly two years.

Sir Iain had come constantly to the house when his Mother was alive and was also a friend of his Father's.

He was an outstanding soldier who had commanded the Scots Greys before he retired.

Talbot could remember long conversations about Scotland.

He thought now that the one person who could help him and give him some idea of what his duties would be as Chieftain would be Sir Iain.

Accordingly, he walked down Piccadilly, past Hyde Park Corner and eventually reached Chapel Street, where Sir Iain lived.

It was a small house crushed between two larger and taller ones.

When he knocked on the door he wondered if

27

perhaps Sir Iain had gone away.

In which case, his visit would be pointless.

It was some minutes before the door was opened.

But, instead of a servant, as he expected, there was a young and very pretty girl who looked at him enquiringly.

"I would like, if it is possible," Talbot said, "to see Sir Iain MacDowall."

When the girl did not reply, he gave an exclamation and said:

"Surely I am not mistaken in thinking you are Tara?"

The girl smiled.

"And you are Talbot Marsham. It is a long time since we have seen you."

"It is indeed," Talbot said, "but after my Mother died I lost touch with many of her friends, including your Father."

"He often spoke of you," Tara said, "but I had no idea after your house was closed where you had gone."

Talbot felt guilty.

He realised it would have been polite, if nothing else, to have called on Sir Iain.

Then Tara MacDowall said:

"If you have come to see Papa, I am afraid you will be disappointed. He . . . died a . . . month ago."

"I am sorry to hear that," Talbot said. "It must have been distressing for you."

"Papa was ill and in pain," Tara said, "so in a way it was a merciful release."

She spoke in a low voice that told Talbot how

much she minded losing her Father.

Then in another tone she said:

"But, please come in. We are talking on the doorstep and, if you are interested, I have a lot to tell you."

"And I have a lot to tell *you*," Talbot said. "That is why I came to your Father for help."

As they were talking, Tara led the way up the narrow stairway to the First Floor.

It consisted of a small Drawing-Room with two windows looking onto the street.

There was also one at the back that looked out over the Mews.

"Do sit down," Tara said, "and tell me why you needed Papa's help."

Talbot sat, and as he did so, he was looking at Tara and thinking how much she had altered.

The last time he had seen her she had looked an untidy sixteen-year-old.

Now, he reckoned she was eighteen, and she had developed into a very lovely young woman.

In fact, he thought, she was far more beautiful than many of the *débutantes* he had seen at the Balls he attended.

"If your Father is dead," he asked, "who is looking after you?"

He knew that Lady MacDowall had died some years earlier.

It suddenly struck him that Tara was not wearing mourning, except for a black sash at her waist.

The house seemed very quiet.

"I am . . . afraid I am . . . alone . . . here," Tara admitted.

"Alone?" Talbot exclaimed. "But that is impossible!"

"It seems strange," she agreed, "but I was informed as soon as Papa died that his pension died with him. As Mama was dead, there was no widow to provide for."

Talbot stared at her in astonishment.

"Are you telling me," he asked, "that you have no money?"

Tara smiled.

"It sounds ... horrifying, does it not?" she answered. "But that is the truth. I am trying to get employment of some sort but finding it ... very difficult."

Talbot frowned.

It was what he had been doing himself, and he knew the difficulties.

He thought it was quite wrong for Tara, who was so young and lovely, to be traipsing round, trying to persuade people to employ her.

"What are you thinking of doing?" he asked,

"I thought I could be a Governess to young children, but the Domestic Bureau to which I went told me that I was too young and far too ... pretty."

She hesitated over the last word and blushed, as if she was embarrassed by what she had to say.

"They were quite right," Talbot said. "It is not the sort of life for you."

He remembered as he spoke how he had always heard that Governesses, if they were attractive, could be the prey of the employer, or his sons.

If they refused to comply with what was demanded of them, they were dismissed without a reference.

"You did not come to talk about me," Tara said, "and I am sure I will find . . . something. Tell me why . . . you are here."

"I came to see your Father," Talbot replied, "because an extraordinary thing happened an hour or two ago."

"What was that?" Tara asked.

"A Scotsman arrived at my lodgings to inform me that my Grandfather, the Earl of Cairnloch, was dead."

"He must have been very old," Tara said. "I remember Papa telling your Mother that he knew him and had actually stayed in his Castle in the North of Scotland."

"He was over eighty," Talbot replied, "but because his only son died a long time ago, my Mother would have inherited the title."

"Oh, yes! Of course she would!" Tara agreed. "In Scotland it can go in the female line."

"That is what I learnt when the senior Elder of the Clan came to see me," Talbot answered. "Finding that my Mother was dead, he then informed me that I am the new Earl and Chieftain of the McCairns!"

Tara clasped her hands together.

"Oh, Talbot, how splendid for you! And how delighted Papa would have been!"

"I can hardly believe it is true," Talbot said, "but what I do know is that I do not know what is expected of me or how I should behave. That is why I came to your Father for help."

"And I know Papa would have been only too willing to give it to you," Tara said. "I remember now, long ago when you and I were talking about Scotland, you said you had never danced the Reels and I told you that you ought to learn them at once."

"I remember that, and I thought at the time it was impertinent of a little chit, as you were then, to give me orders!"

"Have you learnt them since?" Tara asked.

"No, of course not," Talbot replied. "And that is another thing of which I am completely ignorant, besides having no idea of what is expected of a Chieftain when he meets his Clan for the first time. And Andrew McCairn, who came from Scotland to give me the news, tells me I must wear the kilt."

"Of course you must!" Tara agreed. "It would look all wrong for you to be walking about dressed as you are now. Besides, as you well know, all the Clans in the North dislike the English."

"That is something I do know," Talbot said, "considering the way my Mother was treated because she married an Englishman."

"Your Father was so charming," Tara said. "I can understand Lady Janet running away with him. It must have been very, very romantic!"

"It was not very romantic when I discovered that, when my Father died, there was no money. And to tell the truth, I was desperate this morning, wondering where my next meal was coming from."

"And now you are a rich man and very important," Tara cried. "It is like a Fairy Story."

"In which I shall behave like the 'Demon King' unless somebody helps me, and prevents me from making a thousand mistakes so that I don't antagonise everybody the moment I set foot on Scottish soil."

Talbot spoke intensely, and there was a little silence before Tara said:

"I am . . . sure I can . . . help you. Tell me what you . . . want to . . . know."

"You have to help me," Talbot answered, "and you had better start instructing me quickly because, pressed by Andrew McCairn, I am leaving for the North in three days' time."

His eyes twinkled as he added:

"I think the only reason he is waiting so long is that I should have the kilt so that he will not be ashamed of appearing with a Sassenach who has the Union Jack round his neck."

Tara laughed. Then she said:

"Of course you must not do that. I am sure if he can get you a kilt I can find you jackets and sporrans of Papa's which will tide you over until you find a good Tailor in the North."

"That is exceedingly kind of you," Talbot said, "but I have not come here to impose on you."

Then he added quickly:

"But of course! I have just remembered that I now have money and can buy from you anything you are kind enough to let me have."

"Can you imagine Papa allowing that?" Tara

asked. "You know how proud he was. And if it is for Scotland, he would have given you the shirt off his back."

"If we are talking about pride," Talbot said, "the Scottish half of me is very proud, so of course I cannot accept charity, even if it comes from a friend."

They looked at each other, then they both began to laugh.

"This conversation is quite ridiculous!" Tara said. "Of course you may borrow anything you require of Papa's, and when they are no longer useful you can send them back to me."

"And what about the Reels?" Talbot asked. "Are you going to teach them to me?"

"I suppose I shall have to," Tara answered, "but there is not much time. However, you certainly cannot go to the Castle, their Chieftain, having to be a 'wallflower' while the other people dance."

Talbot got up from the sofa and walked towards the window.

He stood with his back to the room, looking out onto the sunlit streets.

He was thinking of the crowd of Clansmen who were waiting for him to come to rule over them.

That was what they expected from their Chieftain.

He wished now with all his heart that he had listened more intently to everything he had ever heard about Scotland.

Because he had thought it unlikely he would ever go there, he had not asked what he realised now were important questions.

He had merely listened to his Mother.

She would tell him how beautiful it was and how much the pipes meant to her.

Then he was aware that Tara had come to his side.

"You must not be . . . frightened," she said. "Papa always said how clever you were, and I am sure you will find yourself doing naturally what is expected of you. Your instinct will tell you what is right and what is wrong."

"My instincts tell me it would be very wrong, from my point of view, not to know a great deal more about the life of a Chieftain than I know at the moment. Do not forget I start at a disadvantage because my Father was English, and they will just be waiting for me to put my foot in it. Especially those relations who have never forgiven my Mother for running away."

"Had your Mother any sisters?" Tara asked. "I have forgotten."

"According to Andrew McCairn," Talbot replied, "there is a sister, Lady Heather, whose son would like to take the place I am to occupy. In fact, he is an applicant for the Chieftainship, but the Elders insisted that my Mother was the rightful heir."

"That is what they would do," Tara said, "and the Elders are very important to you. You must get them all on your side."

Talbot made a helpless gesture, and Tara went on:

"You must first get this man Andrew McCairn to tell you all about them, who they are and what families they have. That will make it easier for you to talk to them when you arrive."

"And what else will happen?" Talbot asked.

Tara reeled off a dozen things he would be expected to understand and know about.

Talbot put up his hands in protest.

"If you think I can absorb all that in a few seconds, you are mistaken," he said. "The only thing you can do is to teach me hour by hour during the few days I remain in London, and I am going to take notes to which I can refer whenever I am at a loss."

"I am sure it will not be as bad as you think," she said. "Of course I will tell you everything you should know, but you must learn the Reels."

She pushed aside one of the armchairs and said:

"Let me show you a few steps now which you have to make in 'Stripping the Willow.' It is going to be difficult for two of us to dance the 'Eight-some,' but at least you can try to remember the movements."

She started to hum the tune to which they could dance to and then showed him the steps.

They were not complicated, and he thought that given the right music and a dance-floor, it would not take him long to become proficient.

He was, as it happened, a good dancer because he was naturally athletic.

He thought, as he danced with Tara, that she was like a piece of thistledown.

She was so light that she might easily float away from him.

They danced round until Tara threw herself down on the sofa.

"There!" she said. "You see how easy it is, and think how magnificent you will look when you are wearing the kilt, the Chieftain's sporran, and a *skean dhu* in your tartan hose."

"That is just the sort of thing I will forget," Talbot said, "and I shall doubtless forget the brooch that pins that piece of tweed, or whatever it is called, to my shoulder."

"Your *plaid*," Tara corrected him, "and the brooch contains a Cairngorm."

Talbot leaned back in the comfortable armchair.

"It is all too much," he sighed. "I think I had better stay in England and leave Scotland to look after itself."

He was speaking jokingly.

Then it occurred to him that if he did stay in England, he would probably starve to death.

Perhaps that also applied to Tara.

He was suddenly aware that she was very thin, and wondered if it was perhaps because of a lack of food.

"When you said you had no money," he asked in a serious voice, "did you mean that this house does not belong to you?"

Tara shook her head.

"Papa rented it twenty years ago when he first married Mama. It has always been our home, although he hoped when he retired we would be able to live in the Country."

"Is not the furniture yours?" Talbot asked.

Tara blushed.

"It is mine," she said, "but I have already sold one or two things and, if I can find somewhere to work, I will, of course, sell the rest."

"You cannot be a Governess," Talbot said. "I do not think it is at all suitable for you. What else can you do?"

Tara put out her hand.

"It seems ridiculous when I have been so well educated, but the woman in the Domestic Bureau was not at all hopeful. "She said I might get a job as a companion to an old lady, or perhaps be a Secretary to somebody who is blind and therefore could not write their own letters. But such cases are very few and far between."

"A Secretary," Talbot repeated. "Tara, I have an idea!"

"What is it?" she asked.

He knew by the expression in her eyes that she was not particularly hopeful that he would come up with anything she would wish to do.

He knew without being told that she was frightened and extremely worried by the position she was in.

Before he told her what he was thinking, he asked:

"Surely, you have some relative who would take you in to live with them?"

"I have thought of that," Tara answered, "but Papa was the only son and had one sister who has been ill for some years and resides in a Nursing

Home. I suppose we have cousins, and certainly a few of them came to Papa's Funeral."

She paused, then continued in a low voice:

"But they did not seem interested in me. I am quite sure they would be horrified by the idea that I . . . might have to . . . live with . . . them."

"Very well," Talbot said. "Now I have an idea to which I want you to listen very carefully."

"Of course I am listening," Tara said, "as I have been ever since you arrived."

"I think actually you have been instructing me and expecting me to listen to you!" Talbot said.

"I was only . . . trying to . . . help," Tara said defensively.

"That is exactly what you were doing, and that is why I want you to go on doing it."

She looked at him in a puzzled fashion, and he explained:

"When Andrew McCairn visited me just now, I could see he was shocked at the garret in which I am living in Half Moon Street. It is an attic for which I pay only a few shillings a week. It was all I could afford."

"Oh, Talbot, have things been as bad as that?" Tara asked.

"Worse," he replied, "but we are not talking about me. What I am telling you is that because I was ashamed of living in such a place, I told Andrew McCairn that I was writing a book and I wished to be alone and very quiet."

"Did he believe you?" Tara asked.

"I see no reason why he should not have," Talbot

said. "But what I am saying is that if I am to be an Author, I need a Secretary."

She stared at him in a bewildered way, and he went on:

"What I am suggesting, and you must admit it is sensible, is that you should come with me to Scotland. You can teach me all the way there, guide me when we arrive, and prevent me from making the more obvious mistakes and having the Clansmen laughing at me."

"You . . . cannot really . . . mean that?" Tara murmured.

"Of course I mean it," Talbot said quickly. "I have been thinking it out, and it is the most sensible thing I could possibly do."

He sighed.

"The more I think about it," he went on, "the less I realise I know about Scotland, Scottish ways, Scottish traditions, and Scottish feuds."

He threw out his hands before he said:

"I know enough about my relatives to realise that I start with a stigma for being half a Sassenach, and a great number of those who follow me because I am a Cairn will be suspicious of my English blood."

"I cannot believe it will be as bad as that," Tara murmured.

"I remember your Father saying once," Talbot went on, "that the Scots never forget. If that is true, and you know it is, they will never forget the Duke of Cumberland—Butcher, as he was called— and the way he punished those who helped the wounded Highlanders by cutting off their hands."

Tara gave a little gasp, but she did not speak, and Talbot continued:

"I am not such a fool as to think that because my Mother was a McCairn they will all look at me with loving eyes or take me to their hearts."

His voice deepened as he said:

"If I am to live in the Castle with McCairns all round me, I have to prove myself and gradually win them over because of the way I behave and because I can make them understand that I really care about them."

"Yes, of course. You are quite right," Tara agreed.

"I am absolutely certain," Talbot went on, "that I shall be unable to do that without your help. Vaguely at the back of my mind when I came here I was thinking I might persuade your Father to stay in the Castle with me until I have 'found my feet' . . . But your Father is no longer here."

There was silence.

Then Tara said in a very small voice:

"Do you . . . really think . . . I could . . . take his place?"

"If you refuse to do so, I know of no-one else. I think your Father was the only Scottish friend my Mother had in England. If there were others, I cannot remember them. What it comes down to, Tara, is that I need you, I need you desperately! If you refuse to help me, I have no idea who else I can turn to."

There was silence until Tara said:

"If you really want me . . . it is the most . . . wonderful thing that could . . . possibly happen. I have been so . . . desperately afraid that . . . when I had . . . nothing else to . . . sell that I would . . . starve. I can hardly . . . believe that what you are . . . saying to me is . . . true."

"It is true," Talbot said, "and, because I admired and respected your Father, I am not going to let you refuse. Your situation is exactly the same as mine was this morning—until Andrew McCairn arrived. By some astounding luck, or perhaps by the blessing of God, we can both be saved."

He moved to stand in front of the fireplace as he went on:

"I know at the back of my mind that when I reach Scotland I shall be sensible and honest enough to realise that if I am a failure, they will somehow manage to throw me out. So I have to succeed, and that means you have to help me."

He smiled before he said:

"If you like, we are two 'Babes in the Wood' and we can only hope the tartan will cover us like leaves and we shall find, when we wake up, the crock of gold at the foot of the rainbow."

Tara laughed.

"I said it was a Fairy Story!"

"And that is exactly what it is going to be," Talbot said. "A Fairy Story in which, with your help, I will win the hearts of those I lead, and somehow both they and we will live happily ever after."

"I can only pray you are right," Tara said, "and you know I will do anything . . . anything in my . . . power to make you the Chieftain they need and a Chieftain they will . . . love and . . . respect."

"In which case," Talbot remarked, "you had better start immediately, for time is running out."

* * *

Talbot did not go to the Countess of Warwick's dinner that night.

Instead, he danced again with Tara in the small Drawing-Room.

Their supper consisted of two eggs, which was all that Tara had in the kitchen, with the exception of some cheese which she had cooked and spread on toast.

Talbot said it was delicious.

"Because I am sure," he said when they had finished their frugal meal, "we have eaten not only your dinner, but your breakfast to-morrow, we will go together to the Hotel where Andrew McCairn is staying. He can provide us with a good breakfast before we go shopping."

Tara showed him her Father's clothes.

Some of them were a little tight for him.

But an evening coat with its silver buttons and jabot, and one Sir Iain had worn in the daytime, would be useful until he had his own.

He guessed, however, that Andrew McCairn would be determined to fit him out with a new wardrobe.

When they arrived at the Hotel in Albemarle Street where Andrew was staying, Talbot knew that Tara was feeling shy.

He had said that he would pick her up, and he

arrived precisely at eight-thirty.

He hailed a hansom cab just before he reached the house in Chapel Street.

It took them to the Hotel where Andrew was staying.

As Talbot paid the driver, he realised it left him with only two shillings in his pocket.

Just for a moment he was afraid that perhaps Andrew had vanished overnight.

Perhaps there was no-one waiting for him and no money either.

Then, before they could enter through the front-doors, Andrew, who must have been waiting, came out to greet Talbot.

" 'Tis fine to see ye, My Lord," he said. "It's guid that ye're not late this morning, as we have a great deal to do."

"That is what I thought," Talbot replied, "and may I introduce you to my Secretary, Miss Mac-Dowall, who is helping me with my book."

He thought that Andrew looked at Tara somewhat questioningly.

Obviously, because she was so pretty, he suspected her chief qualification was not the work she could perform as a Secretary.

Then, when he learnt she was the daughter of General Sir Iain MacDowall, his attitude changed.

As he ushered them into the Dining-Room, he could not have been more effusive or said more flattering things about Tara's Father.

They sat down to breakfast, and Talbot ordered several dishes for himself and for Tara.

He then said to Andrew McCairn:

"I know you will understand that it is absolutely essential for me to have Miss MacDowall with me in Scotland."

There was an expression on Andrew's face which told Talbot he had never imagined this was what he would want.

Talbot went on quickly:

"Miss MacDowall is, of course, helping me with my book, and I could not do it without her. She is also of inestimable help, just as I hope you will be, in telling me what I must do and say as Chieftain of the McCairns."

"Ah had no idea ye might be bringing a young Lady back with ye," Andrew said slowly.

"It is not really a question of my bringing Miss MacDowall," Talbot said, "but of her bringing me! She is a Scot, she knows Scotland well, and even I am aware that the McCairns and the MacDowalls have always been friendly, and at Culloden fought side by side."

He had received this piece of information from Tara only that morning.

It sounded as if he were well informed.

"Ah knew when I came here," Andrew said, "Ah was right about ye, and I know that the Elders will welcome any daughter of Sir Iain MacDowall."

"Thank you," Tara said, "and, as you can imagine, I am longing to be back in Scotland. Papa and I were there last Summer before he . . . became ill. He caught several salmon when the river was low. It made him very happy."

As she spoke, Talbot realised that fishing was another thing he would have to learn how to do.

His Mother had talked about the river that was near the Castle.

He had never had a chance to fish because there was no stream or lake where they stayed when they went to the Country.

They had only a small house on what had been Frederick's Father's Estate.

They kept a few horses there.

Now, Talbot thought, he would have the best horses it was possible to buy when he reached Scotland.

Although he would have to learn how to fish, he was a good game-shot and would not discredit himself on the grouse moor.

At the same time, every moment he was talking to Andrew, or Tara was chatting to him, he thought there was more and more for him to learn, more and more about which he would feel uncomfortable if he did not excel.

It was a relief that Andrew was in a hurry when they had finished breakfast.

He rushed them off to the Tailor, where he said Talbot's kilt was already being made.

"We're fortunate," he explained, "that one of the partners in the shop is a McCairn. He told me he made certain that he always had our tartan in stock beside the more popular ones, like the McDonalds, the Campbells, and the Chisholms."

He paused before he added almost apologetically:

"But you will need, M'Lord, ye'll forgive me saying so, a great many more things than just the kilt."

"That is what I have been telling him," Tara said, "and he will look very smart in them, too!"

"Of that Ah am sure," Andrew said. "He's a fine figure o' a man! The Scots like their Chieftain to look like a man they're proud to obey and follow wherever he leads them."

# *chapter three*

TALBOT walked into Whites Club.

The first person he saw was his friend Henry.

Henry, who was talking to another man, broke off his conversation and moved towards Talbot.

"What on earth happened to you last night?" he asked. "You did not turn up and the Countess was furious!"

Talbot put his hand up to his forehead.

"Good Heavens, how awful," he exclaimed. "I forgot and never thought of it again!"

Henry looked at him in astonishment.

"What were you doing that made you forget?" he asked. "I understood when you left me that you were looking forward to a good dinner."

"I was," Talbot answered, "but then something happened which put everything else out of my mind."

He walked towards the far end of the room and sat down in a chair. Henry sat in another one.

"Will you have a drink?" Henry asked.

"It is on me," Talbot said as he smiled, "and it must be Champagne."

Henry raised his eyebrows.

"What has happened?" he asked. "Has Father Christmas come down the chimney, or have you won a Sweepstake?"

"More or less both," Talbot answered.

He gave the order to the Steward for the most expensive Champagne, which he and Henry had avoided in the past.

Then, before his friend could speak, he drew an envelope out of his pocket.

"Here is five-hundred pounds," he said, "to repay you for what I have borrowed from you in the last few months. I can never thank you enough for your kindness towards me when I most needed it."

Henry took the envelope. Then he said:

"I am completely bewildered, Talbot. Tell me what has happened."

Talbot drew in his breath.

"You see before you," he said, "not your poor, impoverished friend towards whom you have shown great generosity, but the Twelfth Earl of Cairnloch!"

"Are you joking?" Henry asked.

"I have never been more serious," Talbot said. "What is more, and I can hardly believe it myself, Henry, I am a rich man!"

"Start from the beginning," Henry said, "and tell me exactly what has happened."

Talbot had been looking forward to this moment.

He told him how Andrew McCairn had arrived and what he had learnt.

He told him how he himself found it hard to believe that his luck had changed.

"I was thinking desperately after I left you," he said, "that I could not go on for ever scrounging off you and eating properly only when I was asked to a free meal."

"It seems incredible to me," Henry remarked, "that you had no idea that your Mother might have been the Chieftain of the Clan."

"She had a younger brother who apparently died when he was sixteen, although, of course, she was not told of it," Talbot answered. "And now as my Mother's son I am the direct heir to the Earldom and the Chieftainship."

"It is marvellous news!" Henry cried. "And if you do not invite me to come and shoot your grouse in the Autumn, I shall be extremely offended."

"You will be my first guest at the Castle—as soon as I have settled in!" Talbot replied.

He spoke in a more serious tone, and Henry asked perceptively:

"Are you feeling nervous about what will happen when you get there?"

"Of course I am," Talbot answered, "but, by a miracle, I have solved that problem, too."

He told him about Tara, and Henry listened attentively before he said:

"I remember the General. I met him once or twice because he knew my Father. He was a magnificent person and I think everybody admired him."

"Tara, whom I have known since she was a small child," Talbot said, "will certainly be acceptable to the Clan, and she will prevent me from making a fool of myself, which I will certainly do without anyone to guide me."

"Will they not be surprised at your arriving with a young woman?" Henry asked. "Is Tara MacDowall attractive?"

"Very pretty," Talbot replied, "but I suppose, as the Chieftain, I can have whom I like in my own Castle. I have every intention of keeping Tara there for as long as I need her."

He spoke aggressively, as if he were already being confronted with criticism.

Henry laughed and said:

"All right! I am only making a suggestion! You know what the gossips are like about a young and personable man—especially if he is rich and has a title."

"Oh, for goodness sake," Talbot said, "do not make any more difficulties than there are already. Of course I understand what you are saying. But I had no alternative, as the General is dead and therefore could not come with me."

"It is certainly a help that she is the General's daughter," Henry answered a little doubtfully.

"Quite frankly, I know nobody else who is Scottish," Talbot said. "As you will understand, my Father, who adored my Mother, was also very jealous and did not encourage Scottish acquaintances because, he thought, they were blaming him for being English."

"You have often told me how badly your Grandfather behaved in throwing your Father out of the Castle and never speaking to your Mother after she left."

"I have always thought it was an appalling way to behave," Talbot said. "I promise you, it is something I shall never do to my own children, whomever they marry."

"Good gracious me, how things have changed!" Henry exclaimed. "You and I have never spoken of marriage before, having no wish to be fettered to only one woman!"

"I could hardly contemplate such a step without a penny in my pocket," Talbot replied. "Now things are different, and when you come to stay with me in Scotland, I will provide some attractive Scottish girls who will perhaps persuade you to live North of the Border."

Henry held up his hands in horror.

"I cannot imagine anything I would like less," he said. "I will shoot your grouse and catch your salmon, but I am English and I prefer to remain with more civilised people."

"That is an insult," Talbot said, "and if you say something like that in Scotland, I shall doubtless be forced to attack you with my *skean dhu*."

Both men laughed.

The Steward arrived with the Champagne.

He poured it out, and Henry raised his glass.

"To the new Earl of Cairnloch!" he said. "And may you continue, Talbot, to have the luck of the Devil!"

They both drank, then Talbot told Henry of the clothes he had ordered.

"I am going to look really smart in the kilt," he said. "I was fortunate in finding that quite a number of things fitted me in the shop and Tara is lending me her Father's day sporran. She informed me that the Chieftain's sporran will undoubtedly be waiting for me at the Castle."

He paused before he added:

"There are a great many other things waiting for me, including, I hear, another applicant for the Chieftainship."

Henry asked who that was, and after Talbot had explained, he said:

"I should have thought it was rather dangerous to have him living with you, or too near you."

"Why?" Talbot enquired.

"Because, knowing some of the crimes that have happened in Scotland, he will either knock you off the battlements, or drown you in the river."

"You have been reading too many cheap novelettes!" Talbot said. "People do not behave like that these days."

"Not in civilised countries perhaps," Henry said provocatively.

"If you talk like that," Talbot warned, "I shall not have you to stay with me. You will put ideas into the Clansmen's heads which undoubtedly will cause a revolt."

"Or a murder!" Henry teased.

"Oh, shut up!" Talbot answered. "You are trying to frighten me. To tell you the truth, I am quite frightened enough already at the idea of meeting my Clansmen."

He made a grimace before he went on:

"They will undoubtedly be suspicious of my English blood and be looking for me to make mistakes so that they can point the finger of scorn at me."

"It sounds ghastly!" Henry said. "What you must do, Talbot, is to go to Scotland, look at your precious Clan, and, if what you see is unpleasant, come back to England."

Talbot looked at him in surprise, and Henry said:

"If, as you say, you are a rich man, you can go wherever you like. There is no need to sit in an uncomfortable, cold, and draughty Castle having pot-shots taken at you by some young Scot who wants your position."

"I must say, you are a great help in encouraging me to do my duty," Talbot said.

"I am only teasing," Henry confessed. "At the same time, I hate you going so far away."

"Then come with me," Talbot suggested.

Henry shook his head.

"I would like to do that, but I think you ought to 'play yourself in' first, then produce your English friends. You know as well as I do that I have no excuse to wear the kilt."

They both laughed and drank some more Champagne.

Before he left Whites, Talbot could not help telling just one or two other friends of his good luck, and they all congratulated him.

He returned to his lodgings to change for dinner.

He had insisted that Henry should dine with him and meet Tara.

"She has nothing in the house," he said, "and no money, so I had to ask her out to dinner. She is a nice girl, but, of course, being her Father's daughter, she is very proud and I do not think I could give her any money until she is actually working as my Secretary."

"How long is she going to stay with you in Scotland?" Henry asked.

"I made her promise to stay until I feel sure of myself and I am not likely to make a mess-up of anything I undertake," Talbot replied.

"It sounds as if it will be a very long time to me," Henry said. "But I suppose you know what you are doing."

"I am doing the only thing I can do in the circumstances," Talbot said in a serious voice.

He told Henry to meet him at one of the best and most expensive Restaurants in London at eight o'clock.

Then he drove back to Half Moon Street to change into his evening clothes.

He had thought, now that he could afford it, of moving elsewhere.

But there seemed to be no point in doing so for just two or three days.

Quite unexpectedly, he found himself feeling quite fond of his attic lodging.

He knew it was because when he left it he would

be taking a step in the dark.

He had no idea of what was waiting for him after the sea voyage.

The more he heard about the Scots, the more he thought they were a strange, unpredictable race.

They never forgot and never forgave and had fiery passions, like his Grandfather.

They also had a loathing for the English, which would always make him feel uncomfortable.

He stood at the north window, looking out over the roofs.

He was thinking that, despite the poverty of the last years since his Father died, he had enjoyed being with his friends.

Was it wise, he asked himself, to leave all that behind?

He had inherited a title and the Chieftain ship, but from a Grandfather who had never acknowledged his existence.

Almost as if he were being tempted, he thought that, whatever happened, the Earldom could not be taken away from him.

He supposed the money went with it.

If he stayed in England, he could enjoy himself as he pleased.

He could have the horses he had always longed for.

He would be able to entertain his friends who had been so hospitable to him.

It all sounded very attractive.

And yet he knew that if he did such a thing it would be cheating.

It was something he knew he could never contemplate.

"For better or worse," he said, standing at the window, "I go to Scotland."

* * *

Later, Talbot could not help thinking how strange it was when he was host to Henry and Tara.

He was able, without considering the cost, to order the most expensive dishes on the menu.

He thought, too, because he used his new title, that the Head Waiter was more obsequious than he would otherwise have been.

Although he himself was not aware of it, Henry noticed that already he had an air of authority that had not been there before.

Because Talbot thought Tara was tired, he did not linger after the meal was finished, but drove her home.

As she went into the empty house, she thanked him profusely for such an exciting evening.

Then the two friends climbed back into the Hackney carriage and Henry asked:

"Where shall we go?"

"To all the places I have been unable to afford since my Father died," Talbot replied.

They went first to a Gaming Club in St. James's.

Then Henry and Talbot took a hansom cab to a brilliantly-lit building in Princes Street off Hanover Square.

There were two commissionaires outside.

They had a somewhat pugnacious air about them, as if they were ready to throw out anyone who was giving trouble.

They, however, opened the carriage door.

As Talbot and Henry stepped out, one of the men hurried to knock on the closed door of the house.

As they reached it, a small panel was slid aside and two eyes scrutinised them.

The peep-hole was then closed and the door opened immediately.

"Good-evening, Mr. Johnson," a more important-looking attendant said to Henry.

He nodded a reply, and he and Talbot walked down a long, tunnel-like passage and up a flight of carpeted stairs into a large Salon.

There was the clamour of voices and, on a dais at the far end of the room, seated on a velvet canopied throne, was the Madam.

The previous Madam, Katie Hamilton, once the acknowledged Queen of London Nightlife, had arranged the smartest Dance Club in London.

At the back of the house there were a wealth of comfortable, discreet bedrooms.

Each girl had her own for the evening.

When the visitor left, an elegantly dressed maid-servant made the bed and tidied the room.

When Kate had retired some years ago, one of her more intelligent girls had taken over.

Milly Modley was now nearing forty.

She was very unlike her predecessor.

Kate Hamilton had been an enormous, ugly woman.

Her brilliant business sense had made her rich, as well as being the talk of London.

Everybody knew Kate.

She was one of the "sights" for visitors from overseas.

Now Milly sat on the velvet throne and was surrounded by a number of extremely attractive young women.

The male visitors to the Club sometimes asked for them by name.

Alternatively, at a signal from Milly they joined them at the tables at which they were seated.

There were quite a number of tables.

At the same time, across the end of the room there was a large "American Bar."

It dispensed mixed drinks under such names as: "Eye-Openers," "Corpse-Revivers," and "Gun-Slingers."

Talbot knew quite a number of the men standing drinking at the bar.

There was Lord Mohun, once, years ago, the well-known duellist, as well as the incredibly foolish Mr. Bobby Shafto. His claim to fame when young was that he assisted the Marquis of Hastings in letting loose 200 rats on the dance floor of Motts one night.

He was now an old man but still basked in his fame.

Henry, however, seated himself at a table with Talbot and asked for a bottle of Champagne.

Both men knew they would be very foolish to drink anything other than the most expensive.

Even then it was wiser to drink sparingly.

As soon as they had ordered, Milly signalled two of her most attractive girls to join them.

Henry was amused by the one who attached herself to him.

But Talbot suddenly found their rather common voices and cheap scent did not amuse him.

Finally, he put some money down on the table and rose to his feet.

Amid the protest of the two women, they left the Dance Hall.

Only when they were outside did Henry ask:

"What has upset you? Why did you have to leave so soon?"

"I do not know," Talbot replied honestly. "It was just that I thought how shoddy it all was. Those women were such a contrast to Tara, and I had no wish to talk to them."

"Where shall we go now?" Henry asked.

"Personally, I think I will go home to bed," Talbot answered. "It has been a long day, one way or another."

"I have an idea," Henry said. "You must have been asked to-night to a Ball at the Duchess of Richmond's. Let us look in and see what is happening."

Talbot thought for a moment before he replied:

"Very well, but if I am bored I shall leave at once."

Henry did not answer.

He merely told the cab driver where they wished to go and climbed in beside his friend.

"You are becoming very 'high and mighty,' " he remarked. "Perhaps the coronet you can now wear has gone to your head!"

"I never have liked those low places," Talbot said. "I suddenly thought how sordid it was and had no wish to stay."

"I suppose you are right," Henry agreed. "At the same time, it is what you have not been able to afford this past year or so."

"And a good thing too!" Talbot said.

They drove on, and after a moment he said:

"I am sorry, Henry, if I am being difficult. By the way, I have written an abject letter of apology to the Countess of Warwick and sent her some very expensive pink roses."

Henry laughed.

"That is a change. You have not been able to afford a daisy until now."

"I would not have thought of it," Talbot said, "if Tara had not reminded me that the Countess would expect it when I had behaved so badly as to forget her dinner-party."

"Tara is exactly the kind of instructor you should have," Henry commented, "but because she is so pretty, she is going to cause comment wherever she goes, especially when she is attached to your retinue."

"I cannot help that," Talbot said crossly, "so there is no use in your harping on it. I intend to take her to Scotland, and if the Scots criticise me for doing so, I shall ask them whether they will or will not obey me as their Chieftain."

Henry laughed.

"That is exactly what you should do, and it is undoubtedly what your Grandfather would have done."

"There is no doubt about that," Talbot said. "I have been talking to Andrew, who told me that everybody was terrified of him. If he threatened a Clansman with banishment from the Clan for some misdemeanour or other, the man would go down on his knees and beg him with tears running down his face for reinstatement and forgiveness."

"It all sounds very melodramatic and theatrical to me," Henry remarked, "but I imagine you will enjoy sitting in the 'seat of judgement.' "

"Why not?" Talbot enquired.

They arrived at the Duchess of Richmond's large house in Park Lane.

As they went up the sweeping staircase to where she was receiving late guests, Talbot could hear the Orchestra playing in the Ball-Room.

As he and Henry walked in, he thought it was a very different scene from what they had found in the Dance Hall.

The ladies were glittering with jewels.

The *débutantes* in their white gowns were dancing with their partners to a Viennese Waltz.

The scene looked very graceful.

It struck Talbot they were like swans moving over a silver lake.

The Ball-Room was hung with magnificent pictures.

The ceiling was painted a century ago by an Italian Artist.

There were flowers everywhere.

They made the Ball-Room a picture of beauty and elegance.

"This is something I shall remember when I am in the wilds of Scotland," he told himself.

He thought that nothing in Scotland would compare to it.

There were a number of men present with decorations on their evening coats.

The Duchess herself was wearing the famous Richmond tiara.

The tiara was always referred to in the newspapers as being the most outstanding when the Peeresses were present at the Opening of Parliament.

Talbot was standing, admiring what he saw when there was a hand on his arm.

Then a soft voice said:

"You have neglected me for far too long, Mr. Marsham, and I am really very angry with you."

He looked round to see beside him Lady Brompton.

It was almost a year since he had enjoyed a brief *affaire de coeur* with her.

It had come to an end because her husband became very jealous.

She had, therefore, decided that discretion was the better part of valour and told Talbot they could not see each other any more.

He had minded losing her.

This was not because he had been particularly in love, but because it hurt his pride to be more or less turned out of Lord Brompton's house.

He had also been prevented from dancing with Isabel Brompton when they met at other parties.

Now, as he looked at her questioningly, she explained:

"Lionel has been sent by the Prime Minister on a mission to Italy. I was so hoping that I might see you at one of the parties I have had to attend alone."

"You are looking very lovely, Isabel," Talbot remarked as he drew her onto the Dance-Floor.

He thought he had forgotten how gracefully she danced.

She moved a little closer to him as she said:

"I have missed you! Oh, Talbot, I have missed you more than I can possibly say!"

"And I have missed you," he answered automatically.

He thought as he said the words that it was hardly true.

He had recovered from his indignation at being barred from going to Lord Brompton's house or speaking to his wife.

He had soon found that there were plenty of women to take Isabel's place in his life.

He had, however, been piqued at the time.

Now he remembered how soft her skin was and how passionate she had been when he made love to her.

She had an attraction which he found somehow

different from the other women to whom he made love.

Then he asked himself, was it not because Isabel was "forbidden fruit" that he remembered her more vividly than those who had taken her place?

"I always said you were the best dancer I have ever met," Isabel was saying. "We match each other."

The way she spoke and the invitation in her eyes was very obvious.

"Are you really here alone?" Talbot asked.

He had an uncomfortable feeling that her husband might appear at any moment and cause a scene.

"Except for my dinner-party, at which there were eleven other people," Isabel Brompton replied, "but there was no-one with whom I wanted to dance as much as I want to—dance—with you."

There was a slight hesitation before she said the word "dance."

Talbot knew exactly what she was asking.

It occurred to him that there might be no-one in Scotland who would attract him in the same way that Isabel did.

He felt he would be a fool if he refused what the Gods were offering him on his last two nights in London.

"I want to talk to you, Isabel," he said.

He drew her from the Dance-Floor.

They moved through two or three attractively furnished rooms.

At last they found one at the end of the corridor

where they could be alone.

Talbot drew Isabel inside.

On an impulse, as he closed the door he locked it.

He turned towards her and she was waiting, her arms outstretched.

"I have missed you, oh, Talbot, how much I have missed you!" she murmured.

Then he pulled her close against him, and she was unable to speak.

He kissed her until they were both breathless.

When they sat down on a sofa she said:

"I have tried so hard to forget you—but it has been impossible."

"How many lovers have you taken in my place?" Talbot asked.

Isabel shrugged her shoulders.

"Does it matter?" she asked. "I am telling you that I have lain awake at night, thinking of you, and I have looked for you at every party."

"I was thankful if you were not there," Talbot said. "I have not forgotten that you sent me away."

"I had to, oh, darling Talbot, you do realise I had to! Lionel was so madly jealous, and who shall blame him when you are so handsome and so very attractive?"

She raised her lips to his as she spoke.

It was impossible for Talbot not to kiss her again.

He kissed her until at last she said in a whisper:

"Let us go home. It will be quite safe, and I promise you that Lionel will never find out."

For a moment Talbot hesitated.

He thought that if Lord Brompton did create a scandal, it would not be appreciated in Scotland.

Then he told himself that Isabel had no idea of his new status in life.

It would be wise for the moment for her to remain in ignorance.

He stood up and drew her to her feet.

"Let me take you home," he said. "Is your carriage outside?"

*   *   *

It was nearly dawn when Talbot kissed Isabel gently.

"I must go," he said, "before the servants start moving about and there is someone on duty in the Hall."

He had noticed when they had come back last night that there was no night-footman.

He thought somewhat cynically that, if he had not been at the Ball, doubtless Isabel would have brought back somebody else.

He was well aware that, when Lord Brompton was in residence, there was always a night-footman on duty.

He would sit in the padded armchair near the front-door.

Talbot was, however, not prepared to quarrel with Fate for bringing Isabel back into his life.

She had been more exciting and more entrancing than he had remembered.

Their love-making had been very passionate.

He had known, however, when she lay in his arms and whispered in his ear, that she did in fact have a real affection for him.

He was willing to believe it was what she did not have for any other man.

"Must you leave me?" Isabel asked now in a pleading voice. "But, of course, Dearest, there is to-morrow."

"Yes, there is to-morrow," Talbot agreed.

He did not add that the day after he would be on his way to Scotland.

As he dressed himself, she lay back against her pillows.

Her dark hair fell over her white shoulders as her large green eyes watched him.

Only when he had tied his white tie and shrugged himself into his long-tailed coat did she say:

"You must come and dine here. I will ask two older people, who will leave soon after dinner. Then we can be alone."

Talbot knew she was thinking that he could not afford to pay for dinner anywhere else.

She was obviously making it easy for him.

He walked towards the bed.

"Good-night, Isabel," he said. "Thank you for making me so happy."

"It is I who am happy," Isabel replied. "Oh, Talbot, I shall be counting the hours until I see you again to-morrow evening."

He kissed her hand.

She raised her lips and he kissed her forehead.

"Good-night, Beautiful," he said, and moved towards the door.

Isabel threw out her hand as if she would try to stop him at the last moment.

But he went from the room, closing the door softly behind him.

He let himself out through the front-door.

Then he started to walk back in the cool air.

The stars were already receding in the sky, and there was just the suspicion of a faint glow in the East.

As Talbot walked towards Piccadilly he was thinking that he would be with Isabel to-morrow night.

It would be a fitting ending to his old life in London, which he felt was something he might never enjoy again.

He drew nearer to Half Moon Street.

As he did so, he thought he would not tell Isabel of his new title or that he was leaving London for Scotland.

He would give her an extremely expensive present with which to remember him by.

It was something he had never been able to afford before.

Before he left he was paying his debts.

He could also repay a little of the pleasure and the happiness Isabel had given him.

'I will certainly bow out with a flourish,' he thought as he reached Half Moon Street. 'What happens in the next Act is very questionable.'

## *chapter four*

HENRY arrived to collect Talbot from Half Moon Street at nine o'clock in the morning.

He arrived in one of his Father's carriages drawn by two well-bred horses.

There was a coachman, and a footman on the box.

When the Porter told Talbot that Henry was outside, he hurried down the stairs.

When he saw what was waiting for him, he said:

"You are certainly sending me off in style!"

"It was the least I could do," Henry replied. "Where is your luggage?"

"Andrew McCairn has taken it and gone ahead," Talbot answered. "All we have to do is to pick up Tara."

He got into the carriage.

When they sat down Henry said:

"I hope you enjoyed yourself last night."

Talbot smiled.

"It was an appropriate farewell to everything I am leaving behind."

He thought, as he spoke, of how astonished Isabel had been when finally he had told her of his new title and that he was leaving for Scotland.

"You are the Earl of Cairnloch?" she exclaimed. "I cannot believe it!"

"I find it hard to believe myself," Talbot replied, "but it is true, and it means that I shall not see you again for some time."

Isabel looked up at him piteously.

"Oh, Talbot, if only this could have happened before I was married! How happy we would have been together!"

Talbot had to acquiesce.

Yet, at the back of his mind he thought, a little cynically, that the last thing he wanted was a wife who was habitually unfaithful to him.

He did not, however, say so.

He merely gave Isabel the present he had brought for her.

It was an exceedingly expensive diamond broach which he had purchased in Bond Street.

"I shall treasure this always," she said, "but, Dearest Talbot, I find it impossible to believe you are now rich. If only we could put back the clock!"

As this was impossible, Talbot thought it was a waste of time talking about it.

Instead, he kissed Isabel until the flames of passion leapt higher and higher.

Then they could think of nothing but their desire for one another.

Once again, he walked back as dawn was breaking.

As he did so, he thought it was the last time he would sleep in his attic lodgings.

He also thought it was the last time he would make love to Isabel.

Then he told himself impatiently that, if he wished to come to London, he would do so.

Doubtless, anyway, he would need a break from the formality of Scotland.

He would certainly crave the amusements that he had enjoyed during the last two days.

The future seemed to loom before him dark and frightening.

He hurried to get some sleep before Henry would arrive.

He had arranged to take him to Wapping Docks, where Andrew would be waiting on the ship which would carry them North.

As the horses turned into Piccadilly, Henry said:

"After you left me I took Tara out to dinner. I had the idea she had nothing in the larder, and I thought it might be bad for her to start a sea voyage on an empty stomach."

Talbot felt guilty.

"I am afraid I forgot about her," he said. "But I have in fact given her what I said was her first month's salary so that she could settle any debts she owed."

"She told me that," Henry said, "and was extremely grateful for your generosity."

"I would have given her more if I thought she

would take it," Talbot answered.

There was silence for a moment.

Then Henry said:

"I think, Talbot, it would be a mistake to let Tara fall in love with you."

Talbot turned to look at him in astonishment.

"Why on earth should she do that?" he asked. "She has known me ever since she was a child, and she is little more than one now."

"I realise that," Henry said. "At the same time, she has lived a very quiet life during the last two years because of her Father's illness."

Talbot did not say anything, and he went on:

"She is finding it a thrilling and exciting adventure to be going back to Scotland, and, of course, with an attractive man like yourself, who will look overwhelmingly seductive in a kilt!"

"Oh, shut up!" Talbot exclaimed. "You are making me feel embarrassed, and I assure you, while I need Tara to help me so that I do not make mistakes, I have never thought of her as anything but the General's delightful little daughter."

"I quite appreciate your point of view," Henry said. "I was just thinking of Tara's."

"If there are any signs of what you fear," Talbot said, "I shall send her back to London and you can look after her. It will, however, be difficult to find her the sort of job she requires."

"I realise that," Henry said, "and naturally, she is conscientiously thinking of how she can help you, and you will undoubtedly find her indispensable."

"I think, in fact, I have been very clever in making an arrangement which suits both Tara and me," Talbot said. "I cannot think why you should want to make difficulties about it."

As if Henry thought he had said enough, he changed the subject.

They talked of how soon he could come North and stay at the Castle.

He was longing to fish in the River Lochie, which was famous for its salmon.

"You can come as soon as I am sure my Clansmen will not be horrified at my receiving an Englishman. But if they are violent on the subject, you will have to disguise yourself as a Scot."

"Heaven forbid!" Henry exclaimed. "I have no intention of exposing my knees, nor of developing a Scots accent!"

They both laughed at the idea.

They were still laughing when they arrived at Chapel Street.

Tara was waiting with the front-door open.

There were several trunks behind her in the passage.

Because she had no servants, she had been obliged to take them empty down the stairs, then pack them in the Hall.

She thought she had solved rather well the problem of saving Talbot from having to carry them down for her.

She had not expected to see a footman with him.

She was, Henry thought, looking very attractive.

He appreciated that she had been sensible enough

to wear a skirt made of the MacDowall tartan.

There was a neat little green velvet jacket to go with it.

On her head she wore a very becoming green velvet tam-o'-shanter which matched her jacket.

It had a pompom of the same tartan as her skirt.

He noticed there was also a tartan cape lying in the Hall, which she might need if it was cold at sea.

The footman fixed her luggage to the back of the carriage.

They drove off, with Henry sitting with his back to the horses.

"I must congratulate you, Tara," he said, "on looking extremely Scottish, and, when Talbot is dressed as befits a Chieftain, you will be an attractive sight in the Clansmen's critical eyes."

Tara turned to Talbot.

"You are quite sure all your things were ready in time and Andrew has forgotten nothing?"

"You need not worry about that," Talbot replied. "Andrew has been fussing and fuming in case even one small item he ordered was left behind by mistake!"

He smiled and went on:

"He is determined I shall make an immediate impression when we arrive at the Castle. I am quite certain that everything I am wearing now will be dropped into the sea as soon as I take them off!"

Tara laughed.

"Andrew is far too canny with money to do that! He might, of course, use them for a scarecrow, or a

Sassenach 'bogle' for the children."

Henry laughed, and Talbot said:

"Now you see what I am going to have to put up with! I have a very good mind to be thoroughly English and arrive in a frock-coat and my top-hat!"

"That would certainly be disastrous!" Tara said. "Andrew and I will prevent you from doing anything of the sort."

Talbot sighed.

"I knew it was a mistake to take a nagging woman with me! It will be bad enough to have Andrew saying with every other word: 'Ye canna do that,' without you chiming in."

He imitated Andrew's Scottish accent cleverly, and Henry said to Tara:

"There you are, you see. Talbot can talk like a Scot if he wants to. Mind you, make him behave himself or they will either depose or assassinate him and the other applicant for the throne will take over."

"I will look after him," Tara promised.

*    *    *

As the ship moved away from the dock, Tara and Talbot stood waving good-bye to Henry.

He looked very smart as he waved his top-hat to them.

Talbot had a sudden longing to jump ashore and stay in London.

He could now afford a carriage.

He could buy one which was more up-to-date

than the one in which Henry had brought them to the dock.

He could have a London house, where he could entertain his friends.

There would be Isabel, and a great number of women like her, to tell him how handsome he was and excite him passionately.

"Why am I deliberately depriving myself of everything that matters to me?" he asked himself aggressively.

As the ship moved out of the river, Tara said:

"Let us go below and unpack."

For a moment Talbot felt like telling her that he had no intention of putting on his Scottish clothes, not until he reached Scotland itself.

Then he realised that was rather foolish.

The sooner he became accustomed to the kilt the better.

He also had the feeling that his knees, because they had always been covered, would look very white.

The sun and sea breezes would tan them until they were comparable to those of the men who had never worn trousers.

Accordingly, he went below.

The Steamship was a large one.

It carried a great deal of cargo back and forth from London to John-O'-Groats.

Then it called at the Orkney Isles.

It was one of several Steamships of the same type which set off every week.

They returned South with products from the

North which were for sale.

These mostly consisted of lobsters, crabs, salmon, and a great number of crates full of whisky.

There were cabins on board to accommodate perhaps twenty people.

These, Andrew McCairn informed him, were nearly always full.

He had, with difficulty, either by luck or by bribing, managed to obtain four cabins.

There was one for each of them, and the fourth was a substitute Sitting-Room.

"Ah thought ye might wish to be alone," Andrew said solemnly. "It wouldna be right for ye to sit wi' Miss MacDowall in her cabin or she in yourrs. Ah've therefore booked a place where ye can be private or, if ye have a mind, to continue writing your book."

"That is very thoughtful of you, Andrew," Talbot replied, "and I am very grateful."

He then went to his own cabin.

His trunks, which had been brought to hold his new clothes, were waiting.

"I thought perhaps, My Lord," Andrew was saying, "ye might wish tae change before dinner and Ah'll then pack the clothes ye're wearing the noo which ye'll not need on the voyage."

Talbot knew that if it were up to Andrew, he would never need them again.

It made him more determined than ever that the clothes he was discarding would be kept in good order.

He could then don them whenever he wished.

It was just as he had decided that he would return to London whenever he wished.

As Tara disappeared into her own cabin, Talbot began to undress.

He told himself he would feel a fool amongst the other passengers wearing a kilt.

But he had, in fact, noticed that among those who were waving good-bye to people on the dock, at least half-a-dozen men wore the kilt.

Andrew had already undone the trunk which had come from the Tailors.

Talbot took out his newly-acquired clothes.

He could not help appreciating how well they were made and, when he put them on, how perfectly they fitted.

He could, of course, wear the casual tweed coat which had belonged to the General.

He also put on the other sporran, which Tara had told him was correct in the daytime.

The tartan hose was worn only at night.

The natural-coloured stockings made of heavy wool were correct with the heavy brogue shoes that Andrew had chosen for him.

There was a mirror on the back of the door in his cabin.

When he looked at his reflection, Talbot had to admit that he looked unusual, but at the same time a man.

It made him understand that the Scots looked upon their Chieftain as a leader.

It was what he himself seemed to be when he was dressed as a Scot.

A little self-consciously he walked from his cabin into the one next door which had been arranged as a Sitting-Room.

The two bunks were still there, but a table and two chairs had been added.

There was also a sideboard on which there were glasses which in themselves seemed to invite the whisky which a Scotsman would require as a matter of course.

Tara, having discarded her tammy, was sitting at the table, arranging some sheets of paper, a bottle of ink, and some pens.

She looked up as Talbot entered, and said:

"Oh, you do look marvellous! Very, very smart! I think the McCairn tartan is one of the most attractive I have ever seen!"

"I am waiting for you to tell me if I am correctly dressed," Talbot said with a smile.

"You look exactly as I hoped you would," Tara said, "and I know that when you arrive, the McCairns will be thrilled!"

"Do you imagine they are expecting me with top-hat and balloons?" Talbot enquired.

"I would not be surprised," Tara answered. "The Scots suspect the English of doing nothing when they are not fighting, drinking, or running after women and, of course, enjoying themselves."

Talbot laughed.

He sat down at the table and asked:

"What is all this?"

He was looking at the sheets of paper, and Tara said quickly:

"I brought it because I thought it was what Andrew would expect. He has spoken to me about your books, and he is very impressed that you should be writing one. It would be a mistake for him to be disillusioned."

"Then, of course, I must write a book!" Talbot said. "The difficulty will be to choose a subject."

Tara thought for a moment. Then she said:

"I think it would impress your people if you collected some of the legends of Scotland. I am quite sure you could write them in a different way from what anybody else has done before and make them really interesting."

"You flatter me!" Talbot said. "I used to write essays at School, but found it a bore. Once, when I was at Oxford, I kept my diary for a whole year. Otherwise, my writing consists of *billets-doux* to attractive women and letters to the Bank, begging for an increase of my overdraft."

"Perhaps your *billets-doux* could fill a book," Tara replied, "but I wonder who would read them except the ladies who have already received them?"

"They might be useful to instruct young men who find it difficult to string two words together," Talbot said, "which, fortunately, has not been one of my failings."

"Of course not," Tara said, "and I am sure you will have an excellent future. If you ever come South again, you will be able to speak in the House of Lords on behalf of Scotland."

It was an idea that had not occurred to Talbot.

His first idea was that it would be an excellent excuse for coming South.

His second was that he would enjoy speaking to the Members of the House of Lords on a subject that interested him.

He had read his Grandfather's speeches in Hansard.

He had often thought, somewhat impertinently, that there were some on which he could improve quite considerably.

He would make them easier to understand and more colloquial.

He had never thought for a moment that he might have a chance, when he was older, to speak to his peers and be able to hold their attention.

On an impulse he said:

"I tell you what we will do, Tara. We will make notes, or, rather, you will, on what is needed in Scotland and for what they have a reason for grumbling about, as undoubtedly they will, because they are being treated badly by the English."

Tara's eyes lit up.

"You mean you will speak about it and perhaps get a great deal more justice for Scotland than it receives at the moment from Westminster?"

"I make no promises," Talbot answered, "but I might try, and of course you must provide me with the material. It will be your job to listen to what the Elders say. I am sure they will be very long-winded about it, so you must keep a note of it."

"I will do that, of course I will do that!" Tara

agreed. "And I am sure everyone in Scotland will appreciate it if you could change some of the injustices which always infuriated Papa."

They were still talking about it when Andrew came to say that luncheon was ready.

He had had a table arranged for them so that they did not have to sit at the long one with the other travellers.

Talbot realised this was a concession which was given only because the Captain was impressed by his title.

When he came to their table to introduce himself, Talbot realised before he spoke that the Captain was himself a Scot.

His name was, in fact, McTavish, and when he shook hands with Talbot he said:

"Ah'm honoured tae meet ye, M'Lord, an' tae have ye aboarrd ma ship. Ma officers an' I will do everything to mak' ye as comfortable as possible."

"That is very kind of you, Captain," Talbot replied, "and I am very grateful. May I present Miss Tara MacDowall, whom I am sure Mr. McCairn has told you is the daughter of General Sir Iain MacDowall. She is coming to Scotland with me as my Secretary."

He thought the Captain looked slightly surprised at that, and added:

"I am writing a book, and I am also making notes of the many things in Scotland of which I was not previously aware."

"That is verry interesting, M'Lord," the Captain

said, "an' ye've only tae ask if Ah can help ye in any way."

He bowed, and left them to their lunch, which Talbot had to admit was edible, if rather dull.

When they finally finished, the ship was out to sea.

Whilst there was a swell, the sea was not rough, and he and Tara moved briskly round the deck without much difficulty.

He noticed that the other voyagers were all men, except for one old woman who was returning to Orkney.

Talbot realised they were all tradesmen of one sort or another, and in fact rather a dull bunch.

He thought by the time the voyage was over he would be grateful he had somebody like Tara to talk to.

There was also, of course, Andrew, from whom he wanted a great deal of information.

He had, in fact, no idea how large was the Estate he owned, or the Castle.

Or how many McCairns lived within the vicinity.

He found it extremely gratifying to learn that his moors were some of the best on that side of the coast.

The river Lochie was famous for its salmon.

"It stretches for twenty miles," Andrew informed him, "at the top of it there is a loch which the first Earl took as part o' his name."

"I think it is a very romantic name," Tara said, "and Papa always said that the Glen through which the river flows is, in his opinion, one of the most beautiful in the whole of Scotland."

"That is what I want to think," Talbot said, "and what about the Castle?"

It was a question he had not asked before, because, although he did not like to admit it, he was afraid of the answer.

He had a picture in his mind of the roughly-built, gaunt Castles that were part of Scottish history.

He dreaded the rigours of living in a great draughty uncomfortable building with no distractions except the wind howling round the battlements.

He thought of what a purgatory it would be in the long, dark winters.

Andrew, however, smiled.

"Ah'm leaving that as a surprise for ye," he said. "What did your Mother tell ye aboot it?"

"When my Mother talked about her childhood she always made it sound enchanted because she had been so happy," Talbot answered, "so it is difficult for me to separate the truth from her feelings and, of course, her imagination."

"Ah can understand that," Andrew said in his slow way.

"I know Papa was very impressed when he stayed there," Tara chipped in. "I do wish I had asked him more about it at the time. Because he never went to that part of Scotland but visited the MacDowalls who live on the West Coast, I was not particularly interested."

"And what is your Castle like—if you have one?" Talbot asked.

"Rather small, rather uncomfortable," Tara replied. "Yet Papa would rather have been there than in a Palace in any other part of the world!"

"That's what all true Scotsmen feel," Andrew said. "To them there's no place like home. In Scotland there are the moors, the heather, the rivers filled with salmon, and the pipes tae welcome them back."

He spoke as if he were seeing a picture of it all in his mind, which Talbot found very moving.

When Andrew had retired to bed, Talbot said to Tara:

"He is a true Scot from his head to his toes. Do you feel as he does?"

"Of course I do," Tara replied, "and you will feel the same when you have lived in Scotland for a short while."

"I doubt that," Talbot said.

To tease her, he went on:

"I am already longing to hear a Band playing a Viennese Waltz, girls dancing on a well-lit stage, and my Club where the Gentlemen do not speak with a 'burr.' "

Tara gave a little cry.

"You have to forget all that. That was your life because your Mother was exiled. Now you are going back to where you belong."

"I have spent twenty-five years believing I belonged to England," Talbot replied. "I think it extremely unlikely that Scotland will churn up my blood into feeling anything else."

"Oh, it will, it will!" Tara answered. "I am praying, I am praying every night that you will love Scotland and help our people. That they will realise that in you they will have a Chieftain who will lead them into a prosperous future."

Talbot wanted to say that was impossible, but he knew she would not be convinced.

\* \* \*

The next day, when Talbot went into their day cabin, he found that the table had been pushed against the bulkhead and so had the chairs.

He looked at Tara questioningly, and she explained:

"You have to practise your Reels. There are two more I have not yet taught you, and you have to be proficient by the time we arrive."

"You are not thinking that I am giving a Ball?" Talbot asked.

"No," Tara replied, "but they may dance Reels to impress you, and it would be a tremendous feather in your cap if you can join them and show them you can dance as well as they can."

Talbot thought it was a lot of nonsense.

But to please her he struggled with the Reels, one after another, until she said she was sure he would not make a mistake.

They practised the steps over and over again.

He was very quick in understanding what she was trying to show him.

He remembered without any difficulty what he had learnt previously.

"I wish," she said wistfully, "that I could teach you the Sword-Dance."

Talbot was about to say he was relieved to hear she did not know it, when a voice from the door said:

"Ah ken well."

Andrew had been watching them, and now he came in and said:

"Ah used tae dance the Sword-Dance as a laddie and I won prizes at the Games when I was older. Ah'm nae so spry on ma feet, but Ah'll soon teach ye, M'Lord, and it will be something our people will appreciate."

Talbot protested, but Andrew and Tara would not let him refuse.

Andrew found two sticks which he crossed on the floor.

Then he showed Talbot how to dance over and between them.

Tara supplied the music.

After two hours of what Talbot called a strenuous lesson, they told him that he was an excellent Sword-Dancer.

The next two days, as they were moving towards the coast of Scotland, the ocean was very rough.

When finally they reached the North and were not far from Lochie Harbour, Talbot became aware that Andrew was feeling nervous.

For the first time since he had known him, the older man was rather quiet.

It was Tara who said when they were alone:

"Poor Andrew! I know he is not looking forward to having to explain to the Elders, and of course the Clan, that your Mother is dead and that the son of the man who lured her away from them has come in her place."

"With my English blood, I know it was a mistake to try to rule the Scots!" Talbot said.

"You are going to make a magnificent Chieftain," Tara said, "and because you are clever you will appreciate that it is going to take the Clansmen a little time to put aside their prejudices and like you for yourself."

Talbot thought it was going to be just as embarrassing as he had expected it to be.

It was a fine day and the sun was shining when, early in the afternoon, the ship moved into a small fishing harbour at the mouth of the Lochie River.

He was putting the last of his possessions back into his trunk and putting his bonnet comfortably on his head, when there was a tap at the door and Tara said:

"Talbot, Talbot, come quickly! They are all waiting for you!"

"Who are?" Talbot enquired.

"Hundreds of the Clan! Andrew had no idea they would turn out in such numbers! The pipes are playing and this is the moment when you have to make a good impression on them."

She looked at him as she spoke and exclaimed:

"You look very, very smart and very much a Scot!"

"Thank you, Tara," Talbot replied, "and I hope you and Andrew are going to support me, because I think what I am feeling is shy."

Tara laughed.

"I do not believe that, but just be prepared for anything. Andrew did not expect them to gather here, but at the Castle. It is a friendly gesture if they welcome you as soon as you set foot on Scottish soil."

"They may be waiting to throw me into the sea," Talbot remarked.

She looked up at him smiling.

"Not when they see you," she said.

## *chapter five*

THE ship drew into the small port.

Fortunately the tide was high so that they came alongside the Quay and let down the gang-plank.

There was a surge forward of the Clansmen and the pipes grew louder.

"Give them time to get the gang-plank into position," Tara said, "then you go first."

Talbot thought with a smile that she was stage-managing it.

At the same time, it was common sense.

He therefore waited until the seamen had put the gang-plank into place.

There were no other passengers disembarking at Lochie.

They stood on the deck, keeping to one side, curiously watching what was happening.

Slowly and with dignity Talbot walked out onto the deck.

For a moment there was complete silence.

Then a cheer broke out from the back of the crowd and was taken up by those in front.

The pipes started up again, and some children managed to push their way to the front, where they could wave.

Talbot descended the gang-plank.

Waiting for him, who he knew before anyone told him, were the Elders.

He shook them warmly by the hand.

One who was obviously more important than the others said:

"We be here tae welcome ye, M'Lord, as our Chieftain, and assist ye in any way we can as ye tak' ye're Grandfather's place."

"And of course I shall need you," Talbot replied. "You must help me to be worthy of the great honour of being the Chieftain of the McCairns."

His voice rang out.

Most people could hear what he was saying above the skirl of the pipes and the noise of the crowd.

They were obviously pleased at what he said.

Then Talbot began to shake hands with everybody he could reach.

While he was doing so, Andrew and Tara came down the gang-plank.

Tara was introduced to the Elders, who were clearly impressed that she was her Father's daughter.

By the time she had met at least a dozen people, Talbot was moving through the crowd.

He was shaking their hands and talking to everyone he could.

He then found at his elbow Andrew, who said:

"Ye should move awa' noo to the Castle. There'll nae doot be more of the Clan there with their women and children."

Talbot nodded.

"How do we get there?"

"It's no more than aboot half-a-mile awa', and if ye walk on ahead, we'll all follow ye."

The Pipers were on either side of him as Talbot walked to the end of the Quay.

Tara was escorted by Andrew as they made their way to the Castle.

After them came everybody who had come to meet the new Chieftain.

Having left the port, there was a road up onto a low cliff.

It had fir trees on either side of it and now, in the distance, Talbot could see the Castle.

It was impossible for him to speak above the noise of the pipers.

Anyway, it was obviously expected that he walk alone.

As he drew nearer, he could see that the Castle was quite different from what he had imagined.

He thought it would be built of grey stone.

Instead, it was almost white and surmounted by towers and turrets.

It had not only an impressive look, but also a very attractive one.

He realised as he drew nearer still that the Castle had been built on high ground.

Below it was a garden which ended in a low wall,

and beyond that there was the sea.

The Castle stood in a bay of its own.

Talbot thought that nothing could be more attractive or more different from the cold, rough stone building he had expected.

As the trees came to an end, he saw that behind the Castle there was a huge Court-yard.

It was filled at the moment with Clansmen, women, children, and dogs.

They had been made aware of his arrival by the sound of the pipes.

When he appeared, a great cheer went up.

At the same time, another dozen Pipers joined in playing the same tune.

Talbot guessed it belonged to the Clan and might be their battle song.

It was then Andrew was at his elbow.

He directed him to where, in the midst of the crowd, he could see there was a small dais.

On it was a chair made of stags' horns.

As he walked towards it, he could see behind it were a number of other chairs also made of horn.

They were not as elaborate as his own, but were for the Elders.

He walked onto the dais, and stood with all the pipes playing, while the Clansmen cheered.

Then he sat down in what he knew was the Chieftain's seat.

First, the Elders came one by one to swear their allegiance.

They went down on one knee in front of him and kissed his hand.

As they did so they swore to serve him obediently, both in peace and war and in life until death.

It was fortunate that Tara had described the ceremony of loyalty to the Chieftain while they were at sea.

Talbot therefore knew what to expect.

When each man who had made his obeisance rose to his feet, Talbot spoke to him.

When the Elders had all sworn their allegiance, there were others.

Talbot understood they were either Land-owners or else had positions of importance in the Clan.

The ceremony took a long time.

Talbot was wondering how many more men would come on the dais, when Andrew came behind his chair to say:

"That is the end. Now Your Lordship must say a few words."

Talbot rose to his feet.

He then made what Tara thought was an excellent speech.

He thanked everybody who had come to welcome him.

He told them how proud he was to be standing on the land of which his Mother had so often spoken.

He then promised to lead, support, and serve those who relied on him.

He asked them all to help him so that he could be worthy of those who had preceded him, those who had made the McCairn name important all through the history of Scotland.

When he had finished, some of the people clapped and a great number cheered.

Talbot stepped down from the dais.

As he did so, he could see by the expression on Tara's face that she was proud of him.

It was then he understood that he could go into the Castle.

He walked towards the front-door, where there were a number of servants, all wearing the kilt.

"The Elders will leave you now," Andrew whispered.

Talbot stopped and turned round.

The Elders were just behind him, and he said:

"I would like to see you all to-morrow morning, if that is convenient. Will you come here at about eleven o'clock and you can tell me what are the most urgent matters to be attended to now that I have taken my place as your Chieftain."

The Elders were delighted by the invitation.

Once again Talbot shook them by the hand.

At last he was able to enter the Castle, and Tara and Andrew came with him.

He was introduced first to the servants.

Then, as he went through the outer Hall, he saw an even larger one.

It had a wide wooden staircase on one side of it.

It was then Andrew said to him:

"Lady Heather and Mr. Alastair McCairn will be waiting for Yer Lordship in the Drawing-Room. Will Ah come wi' ye, or would ye rather meet them alone?"

"I think you should accompany me," Talbot replied, "and introduce Miss MacDowall, whom they will not be expecting."

They walked to the top of the stairs to where there was a large landing.

A servant opened the door of the Drawing-Room.

It was a very attractive room with three high windows looking out over the sea.

Over the mantelpiece was a huge portrait of Talbot's Grandfather, the late Earl.

One wall was covered with books, encased behind glass panels.

Talbot, however, had eyes only for the woman sitting by the fireplace.

There was a young man standing behind her chair.

Talbot had expected his Aunt in some way to resemble his Mother.

To his surprise, she looked older.

She also had none of the beauty which his Mother had retained until she died.

As he walked towards her, she rose slowly to her feet.

He knew before he reached her that there was a hostile look in her eyes.

Talbot held out his hand.

"How do you do, Aunt Heather?" he said. "My Mother often spoke about you, but I never expected I would come to Scotland and meet you."

"And we certainly did not expect you!" Lady Heather said harshly. "I was extremely surprised when I learnt that your Mother was dead and that you had accepted the position as Chieftain that she is unable to occupy."

There was no doubt that Lady Heather was speaking in an aggressive tone.

Talbot did not reply.

Instead, he turned towards her son.

"I think you must be my Cousin Alastair," he said.

"That is right," Alastair replied. "I thought you would be enjoying yourself too much in London to want to come here."

"As I now have my Grandfather's title, of which the Lord Lyon, King of Scottish Heraldry, will no doubt fully approve," Talbot replied, "it would have been very remiss not to come and see where my ancestors have lived for so many years, or to have neglected the Clansmen who have followed them so faithfully."

As he turned back, Andrew said to Lady Heather:

"May I, My Lady, introduce Miss Tara Mac-Dowall, who has accompanied His Lordship to Scotland to—"

Before he could continue, Lady Heather interrupted, speaking to Talbot:

"If you have brought your fancy woman with you," she said rudely, "I have no wish to meet her. Either she withdraws from this room, or I do!"

For a moment Talbot felt like raging at his Aunt.

Instead, with admirable self-control he said quietly:

"You are making a most unfortunate mistake,

Aunt Heather. Miss MacDowall is the daughter of General Sir Iain MacDowall, who has stayed here with my Grandfather and who was a great friend of my Mother's. He would, I know, have accompanied me to Scotland if he had not died a month or so ago."

He paused before he continued:

"With great kindness, because I had so much to learn about Scotland and its people, Miss MacDowall took her Father's place. It was only thanks to her instruction that I was able to carry out the ceremony which has just taken place outside without making any mistakes."

As he finished speaking, there was an uncomfortable silence.

At last Lady Heather said grudgingly:

"If I have made a mistake, I must of course apologise. How do you do, Miss MacDowall!"

She held out her hand, and Tara took it, at the same time dropping her a small curtsy.

"I know how much my Father would have liked to come with His Lordship," she said.

Alastair, who was obviously impressed by Tara's appearance, said:

"Well, I think it was exceedingly kind of you to take his place. Do you live in London?"

"My Father had a house there when he was commanding the Scots Greys, and when he retired he kept it on, finding it convenient when he was not in Scotland."

There was no doubt from the way Tara behaved and spoke that she was a Lady.

Lady Heather without an effort said:

"I am sure, Talbot, you and Miss McDowall will like some tea, and perhaps Mr. McCairn will join us?"

Because Andrew was embarrassed by this uncomfortable exchange between relatives, he said quickly:

"Ah thank Yer Ladyship, but Ah came only to help His Lordship tae find his way, and if ye'll excuse me, Ah'll awa' hame."

Talbot turned round.

"Of course I understand you will want to get back and see your family," he said. "I can never thank you enough for all your kindness, or indeed for finding me when you learnt that my Mother was dead."

He smiled before he went on:

"As the Elders are coming here to-morrow at eleven o'clock, I should be grateful if you could see your way clear to coming at ten-thirty so that we can talk over various matters before they arrive."

It was obvious that Andrew was gratified by this invitation.

As Talbot shook his hand he said:

"Ah thank ye, M'Lord, and may God bless this Castle noo that it's yourrs, and ye ken that like ma kinsmen Ah'll be always at yer service."

Talbot walked with him across the room and out to the top of the stairs.

He then said in a low voice:

"You are leaving me in the lions' den, Andrew. Are they staying here in the Castle?"

"Aye, they are," Andrew replied in a whisper. "They have been living here ever since yer Grandfaither died. Your Lordship'll find it harrd to be rid of them."

Talbot nearly replied that he should have been made aware of this before.

Then he knew that, even if he had known about it, there would have been nothing he could do.

He went back into the Drawing-Room.

Lady Heather had moved to where a table was laid for tea.

On it was a large silver tea-pot, a kettle, and a cream jug all arranged on a vast silver tray.

She was sitting in front of it, pouring tea into the china cups.

There was, he thought, enough food on the table to feed a Regiment of soldiers.

As he joined her, he saw that his Aunt was looking sour.

Alastair, however, was talking animatedly to Tara.

The conversation ceased as Talbot sat down and his Aunt passed him a cup of tea.

"Did you have a good voyage?" she enquired.

"We were fortunate that the sea was not rough, and as Miss MacDowall and I had a great deal of work to do, neither of us, luckily, suffered from sea-sickness."

"Work to do?" Lady Heather questioned with a sharp glance at Tara.

"I am writing a book," Talbot said in a lofty manner, "and, as Miss MacDowall did a great deal of secretarial work for her Father, she is helping me."

"And what is the book about?" Lady Heather enquired.

"Scotland," Talbot said briefly.

"Of which you know nothing!" she said, and it was a challenge.

"I may not have visited Scotland," Talbot replied, "but you can imagine that, as my Mother could not speak to my Father of the place where she was born and the country she loved, she talked to me."

He looked up at the bookcase as he went on:

"I have also read a great many books—both at Oxford and since I have grown up—about Scottish history. I am therefore well aware of how this country has suffered under the English and how much there is to do now to bring back both peace and prosperity."

Lady Heather stared at him in astonishment, and Andrew said:

"That is jolly good! I am sure Miss MacDowall will help you find all the right things that you should write about."

"Of course I will," Tara said quietly. "And my Father often wished that he had time to do more for Scotland than he was able to do when he was involved with the Regiment."

They went on talking until, as tea finished, Talbot said:

"I understand, Aunt Heather, you are staying at the moment in the Castle."

"Yes, I am!" she replied sharply. "You will need a hostess. Alastair and I moved here after my Father died to make sure everything was kept in the right order. One can never trust servants, however long one has had them."

"I should have thought," Talbot said stiffly, "that as most of the men whom I met downstairs must have been here with my Grandfather, they are both loyal and trustworthy."

His voice changed as he continued:

"However, now that I have arrived, I would prefer to run my Castle in my own way as soon as I know my way about it."

He turned as he spoke and said to Tara:

"I think first of all we must explore the Castle and find, of course, where we are both sleeping. Then, Aunt Heather, we will meet you here before dinner."

For a moment he thought she was going to challenge the way he was supplanting her in giving the orders.

However, after her lips had tightened, she said in a somewhat reluctant tone:

"Alastair and I will go to our own Sitting-Room and, as you say, meet you here before dinner, which is usually at seven-thirty."

"Very well," Talbot said. "We will leave it like that for to-night, but I find it is a somewhat early hour to dine, especially in the Summer."

Lady Heather swept from the room.

She was followed reluctantly by her son, who was having a last word with Tara.

As the door shut behind them, Tara said in a whisper:

"You were splendid! Absolutely splendid! At the same time, she is your . . . enemy."

"I realise that," Talbot said, "but I am not going to be pushed about just because she wants that beardless boy put in my place."

He walked across the room to the fireplace.

After a moment's pause, Tara moved to join him.

"I was just thinking," she said, "that if you try to turn her out, she might make it very uncomfortable for me to stay here."

"What do you mean by that?" Talbot asked.

"I had not thought of it before, but if you treat me as my Father's daughter and not exactly as a paid Secretary, I should have a chaperon."

Talbot remembered what Henry had said to him, and frowned.

He had been determined to think of Tara as little more than a child.

It had therefore struck him that, as a young woman and of course a Lady, she should have a chaperon.

"I see your point," he agreed after a moment. "So we shall just have to wait and see what happens, but personally, I have no wish to have my Aunt undermining my authority."

He looked at Tara as he continued:

"She is probably hoping I will have a stroke and die."

"You are not likely to do that," Tara said. "At the same time, there is hardly a Castle in Scotland in which a crime has not been committed, usually so that the present Chieftain can be replaced by somebody else."

"You are not to frighten me," Talbot said quickly, "otherwise I shall send you straight back to London, and the book we are supposed to be writing will never see the light of day."

Two dimples appeared on either side of Tara's mouth.

"Now you are threatening me," she said, "and of course to lose your book would be a catastrophe."

They both laughed.

Then Talbot pulled the bell-rope.

"Now," he said, "we are going to explore the Castle, and the person who is going to show it to us is not my Aunt or my Cousin, but the Butler, unless of course there is a Curator, which I doubt."

"Andrew told me," Tara answered, "that Ross, the Butler, was in fact your Grandfather's personal servant and had been with him for nearly thirty years."

"Then that is the man we want," Talbot said.

By the time that Talbot went to dress for dinner, he and Tara had been all over the Castle, right up to its highest point.

They had been out on the battlements from which they had a magnificent view of the sea.

Talbot was entranced by all he saw in a way he had never expected to be.

To begin with, he had never imagined that the Castle would be so well furnished.

It had pictures which would have graced any Museum in the South and a collection of silver which had been handed down from generation to generation.

The furniture, too, was surprising in that it had come, not as he had feared from heavy-handed local craftsmen but, surprisingly, from all parts of the world.

There was French furniture.

It had been brought to Scotland at the time the aristocrats were being guillotined.

Their possessions had been sold by the Revolutionaries.

There was furniture from Germany and Austria, besides pictures from Italy.

He could hardly ask the Butler how it was possible that the McCairns had such good taste.

Then he learnt that his ancestors had travelled a great deal.

Also, he remembered his Mother telling him that a number of them had been Diplomats.

They had served in many European countries.

They had certainly brought home a great many mementoes.

The Castle was, in many ways, a Museum.

There was, of course, a profusion of stags' heads and ancient weapons that had been used by the Clansmen when they went to war.

There was also a Gun-Room filled with the latest sporting guns and a number of interesting ancient duelling pistols.

When the tour was finished, Talbot knew that

the old Butler was amused by his astonishment at everything he saw.

He thanked Ross and said:

"To-morrow I would like to talk to you about the times I want the meals served. Also I would like you to introduce me to the Cook and all the Senior servants in the Castle."

"Ah'll do that, M'Lorrd, an' thank ye," Ross replied.

He was obviously getting on for seventy, but he moved quickly.

He had dead white hair, but Talbot was sure he could carry on his duties for a year or so.

He knew he would be of great help if he was on his side as the new owner of the Castle.

Ross had shown Tara her bedroom, and they found two maids unpacking her trunks.

Talbot was, of course, sleeping in the Chieftain's Room, which was very impressive.

It had a tower at one end of it, with three windows looking out towards the sea.

There was a huge four-poster bed facing a magnificently carved marble fireplace which had come from Italy.

On the walls were portraits of his ancestors.

The furniture was inlaid walnut with the coat of arms of the McCairns engraved on the handles.

"Ah've chosen Euan, M'Lorrd," Ross informed him, "tae be Your Lordship's Valet and Ah hope he'll be to your satisfaction."

Talbot thought of how he had been unable to afford a valet for the last three or four years.

It would be a joy to be looked after again.

He shook hands with Euan, who was a strong-looking man with, at the same time, an intelligent expression.

"Any wee thing Yer Lordship wants, ye have only tae ask him," Ross said.

"I am very grateful to you," Talbot replied, "and I hope you will tell me everything you think I should know as regards the running of the Castle and the people who serve in it. I know I can rely upon you and I would appreciate complete and utter frankness."

He knew by the expression on Ross's face that he had said the right thing.

As the old man left, he said to Euan:

"That applies also to you, as I shall be seeing more of you than I will any of the other staff. I hope you will be frank enough to tell me if you think I am doing anything wrong or upsetting anybody unnecessarily."

He smiled before he said:

"You are of course aware, as everybody else is, that I am stepping into a new world and a country in which I have never been before."

"Ah'll see that ye know a' ye need to know, M'Lorrd," Euan replied.

The two men smiled at each other.

In his dress kilt and jacket, with a lace jabot at his throat, Talbot reached the Drawing-Room before anyone else was present.

Outside the sun was sinking, and the light on the hills on either side of the bay was very beautiful.

The sea was calm and glimmered with various shades of green.

It was so lovely that Talbot drew in his breath.

His Mother had often told him how beautiful Scotland was.

But no words could describe what he saw at this moment.

As if for the first time, he realised that it was his.

He looked down into the garden below, where a fountain was playing.

Skilfully arranged were flower-beds that reminded him of the gardens he had seen in France.

Then he looked again at the moors to his right and left.

The sky, pale above the sea, was darkening as it went higher.

"How can this have happened to me?" Talbot asked himself.

The door behind him opened, and he knew without looking round that Tara had come in.

He did not turn, and she came to his side.

For one second she did not speak.

Then she said softly:

"It is yours . . . all yours!"

"That is just what I was thinking," Talbot replied, "and wondering how I could have been so lucky."

"And I have been thinking," she said, "that you are the right person in the right place at the right time, and there is a great deal you can do here."

"For the moment, I am only entranced by what I see," Talbot answered.

Before he could reply, the door opened again and he heard Lady Heather say sharply:

"So here you are, Talbot! I hope you enjoyed your tour of the Castle. There are a great many repairs that need doing which I wish to talk to you about."

Reluctantly, Talbot turned from the window.

His Aunt was looking, he thought, even more ugly and unpleasant.

She was standing on the hearth-rug.

Alastair, who had obviously followed her into the room, was walking towards Tara as if drawn by an invisible magnet.

"Ross showed me everything I wanted to see," Talbot replied. "I was appreciating the excellent taste of our ancestors rather than looking at anything in a critical manner."

"Then the sooner you get down to hard facts, the better," Lady Heather said in the same sharp voice. "I wished to give the order for a number of things to be repaired or replaced. But I was told that nothing could be done without the Chieftain's authority. Now that you are here, I will give a list of all the things that should be done."

"That is very kind of you," Talbot replied, "and of course I will give my attention to any suggestions you may make, but will decide for myself what is most important."

Lady Heather glared at him angrily.

Then, when she would have opened her lips as if to say something unpleasant, she changed her mind.

"Of course, Talbot, that is your prerogative," she said, "but having lived here for most of my life, I know exactly what is necessary and what is not, who is trustworthy and who should be dismissed, or—retired."

As she said the last words Ross appeared at the doorway.

There was no doubt to whom she was referring.

"Dinner is served, M'Lorrd," he said in a courtly manner.

Talbot proffered his arm to his Aunt.

"May I take you in?" he asked.

She was obviously surprised, but she rested her fingers lightly on his arm.

They walked through the doorway, followed by Alastair escorting Tara.

As they reached the Dining-Room, Lady Heather said:

"To-night we are only four, as I thought you would be tired, but to-morrow I have asked a party of neighbours whom it is important you should meet, and several of our relatives, who are coming from long distances to stay in the Castle."

Talbot drew in his breath.

He knew it was too soon to wish to entertain.

He was aware that once again his Aunt was asserting her authority.

He wanted to tell her that she had no business acting in such a manner.

Then he knew it would be impossible to put off the guests at the last moment.

It would only make trouble, and there was no alternative, therefore, but to accept the party that had been arranged.

"I would like a list of everybody who has been invited, first thing to-morrow morning," he said, "and as regards our relatives, I would appreciate if you would explain exactly who they are, their interests, and where they come in the Family Tree. I suppose we have one somewhere in the Castle?"

"Of course," Lady Heather replied. "It hangs on the wall in your Grandfather's Study."

Talbot remembered vaguely that he had seen it when Ross had shown him the Study.

"I will study it to-morrow," he said, "but, of course, I wish there were a little more time before those who appear on it are my guests."

"I naturally assumed," Lady Heather said in a spiteful tone, "that after all the gaieties in London, you would find the Castle very dull unless it was full of chattering people, with whom I am sure you have spent most of your time."

"I spent most of the time with my Mother when she was so ill," Talbot replied coldly. "I can assure you that her friends were not just chatterers, but people like Sir Iain, who had positions of importance, and all of whom were extremely interesting and informative."

It was a rebuke, and Lady Heather was aware of it.

She glanced across the table to her son, who was talking to Tara, being very animated as he did so.

There was a hard look in her eyes which Tara noticed.

Then Lady Heather lapsed into a silence which she made no effort to break as the dinner progressed.

When the last course had been served, there came the faint sound of the pipes.

It grew louder and louder until finally the Piper came into the room, playing "The Skye Boat Song" as he walked round the table three times.

When he stopped playing, he stood beside Talbot's chair and saluted him.

Fortunately, Tara had told Talbot what was expected.

Ross had already put in front of him the quaich, a boat-shaped goblet which contained neat whisky.

Talbot rose and presented it to the Piper, who said the traditional words in Gaelic before he drank the whisky.

Saluting Talbot once again, he went from the room.

As he sat down, Lady Heather looked at him in surprise.

"Did your Mother tell you that the Piper always plays round the table of a Chieftain?"

"Of course she did," Talbot said. "It is something I have known since I was a child."

He spoke as if he thought his Aunt was very ignorant to have supposed otherwise.

Then, as if she felt she must be disagreeable, Lady Heather said:

"And what did your Father, who was English,

think about so much talk about Scotland? He must have resented it?"

"My Father loved my Mother and wished her to be happy," Talbot said. "I think, Aunt Heather, it would be a great mistake to keep referring to him now that I have come to Scotland and taken my Mother's place."

He paused to say more quietly:

"She was ideally and completely happy with my Father. She would want me now to emulate my Grandfather and my ancestors before him, and to do that I must be Scottish and think only of Scotland, which is where I belong."

He thought as he was speaking that, if she had dared, Tara would have applauded him.

But he knew that both his Aunt and Alastair were staring at him as if they could not believe what they had heard.

At the same time, some perception told him that there was more behind their attitude than appeared on the surface.

It was ridiculous, and yet he had the strange idea that they were plotting something.

What it could be he had no idea.

# *chapter six*

TARA went into the Breakfast-Room to find there was nobody there.

She was just helping herself from a dish of white fish fresh from the sea, when Talbot came in.

He had two dogs at his heels.

Looking round, Tara smiled at him.

Yesterday he had discovered that his Grandfather's dogs had been shut up in kennels ever since he had died.

When he released them, they were so thrilled to be free that they followed him everywhere.

Tara was certain they had slept by his bed to keep guard over him.

"Good-morning, Tara," Talbot said, "I see we are the only 'early birds.' "

"I think you have been outside," Tara answered. "It is a lovely day."

"I have been down to the sea," Talbot answered, "and I have never seen anything so beautiful as the colours on the water and the light on the hills."

She smiled at him.

"I thought you would think that. There is nowhere in the world that has such wonderful lights as Scotland."

Talbot helped himself from two different dishes, walked back to the table, and sat down.

As he did so, the door opened and a servant came in, carrying something on a plate.

He put it down beside Talbot, saying:

"Her Ladyship—M'Lord, asks me tae tell ye she's a headache the morn, but she sends ye a haggis she cooked hersel' yesterday."

"Thank you," Talbot said. "Tell Her Ladyship I am sorry to hear that she is not well."

The man went from the room, and Tara said:

"I have never seen that man-servant before."

"He comes from my Aunt's house," Talbot explained, "and is always in attendance on her, or, rather, Alastair."

Tara thought there was something strange about him, but she did not say so.

Talbot looked at the haggis which was not large.

He pushed it a little to one side and said:

"I do not want to insult you or your Scottish customs, but I have no wish to eat a haggis at breakfast-time."

Tara laughed.

"As it happens, nor have I. It is far too heavy. But as your Aunt has cooked it for you especially, perhaps she will be offended."

Talbot considered this for a moment.

"I have an idea. If we do not appreciate it, the dogs will, and they can save my face when she asks me if I enjoyed it."

Tara laughed again.

"That is a good idea. I am sure *Thistle* and *Roger* will be delighted."

Talbot cut the haggis in half and threw it to the dogs.

They were lying on the hearth-rug in front of the fireplace as if that were their usual position.

They gobbled the pieces of haggis up quickly, then lay down again.

"They are beautiful dogs," Tara said. "I have always loved Labradors, and Papa had one for years. When he died I wept bitterly."

"I think these two will be happy with me," Talbot said. "They certainly seem to have accepted me as their Master."

"As we all do," Tara said with a twinkle in her eyes.

They talked and laughed as they ate their breakfast.

They were just finishing it when the man-servant who had brought the haggis again came into the Breakfast-Room.

He went to Talbot and said in a tense voice:

"Mr. Alastair asks ye, M'Lorrd, if ye'd come up to th' North Tower. He's something tae show ye, and it's verry urgent. He asks if ye'll come alone."

Talbot raised his eye-brows.

Then, as he was about to say something scathing, he thought it would be a mistake in front of the man-servant.

He merely nodded his head and waited until the man-servant withdrew.

Then he asked Tara:

"What do you think this is about?"

"I expect he has found something that needs repairing," Tara replied.

"My Aunt showed me at least half-a-dozen things yesterday which she wished done immediately," Talbot said, "but I refused to hurry in giving orders until I understand how the whole Castle is run and at least who tackles the repairs."

"I am sure you are wise," Tara said, "but you had better go and see what your Cousin wants."

"I suppose so," Talbot sighed. "He said it was urgent."

He rose from his chair and walked towards the door.

When he had gone, Tara sipped her coffee and then heard a sound behind her.

She turned her head.

To her surprise, neither of the Labradors had followed Talbot.

She thought it was strange.

Then, when she looked at them, she realised they were asleep and what she had heard was one of them snoring.

She got to her feet and, going towards the fire-place, she said:

"Come on, boys! Come for a walk with me until your Master gets back."

Neither of the Labradors moved.

She stared at them.

It was very strange that they did not respond. Then a sudden thought struck her.

It seemed impossible, and yet she turned and ran from the Breakfast-Room, nearly knocking over Ross, who was just outside the door.

"The North Tower!" she said. "Which way is it?"

For a moment she could not think in which direction she was facing.

"To yer left, Miss," Ross replied.

Tara was already running, and he stared after her in astonishment.

She tore down the corridor and up the stairs at the end of it.

When she reached the Second Floor, there was another staircase leading upwards.

She remembered now that, when they had gone round the Castle with Ross, he had taken them to both the North and South Towers.

There was another long passage.

At last she reached the narrow steep stairs which led up to the Tower itself.

Just before she reached them she saw on the wall an arrangement of ancient weapons.

She had also seen them in other parts of the Castle.

There was a Clansman's shield, and round it were swords and dirks that had been used long before there were rifles.

Hardly thinking of what she was doing, instinctively she pulled the nearest dirk off the wall.

She then hurried up the steps to the Tower.

\* \* \*

Talbot, when he had left the Breakfast-Room, had walked without hurrying himself along the passage and up the steps which led to the Tower.

He thought it was very tiresome of Alastair to send for him in such an imperious manner.

He was thinking, as he had before, that the sooner his Aunt and her son went back to their own house, the better.

He had learnt from Ross that it was up the Glen and about ten miles away.

It was near the river, and the moor behind it had belonged to the McCairn whom Lady Heather had married.

He had been an elderly man and she was still young.

He had died over five years ago.

"Her Ladyship finds being so far doon the Strath very boring," Ross had said. "She was always drivin' up tae the Castle when his late Lorrdship was alive, tryin' tae persuade him tae have her an' Master Alastair as his guests."

"As my Grandfather was lonely, I wonder he did not agree," Talbot answered.

"Nae, nae, there were reasons, verry guid reasons, M'Lorrd, why His Lorrdship said 'No' every time she suggested it."

Talbot was listening as the old man went on:

"At times he let her bide here at Christmas or the New Year, but His Lorrdship always sent them awa' after they'd been here a day or two. Ah thinks he got bored wi' Her Ladyship's complaints an' in the Servants' Hall we were always glad tae see her go."

The way Ross spoke told Talbot that the servants had no liking for his Aunt.

He thought again that the sooner he turned her out the better.

At the same time, however, he was aware that Tara needed a chaperon.

There was no use pretending she was just a Secretary when she was the daughter of Sir Iain.

Anyone only had to look at her to realise how attractive she was.

In fact, "lovely" was the right word, he told himself.

He could, of course, once he had established himself, send Tara away, too.

But that was something he had no intention of doing.

"I want her here," he told himself firmly. "I need her, and all the old gossips can talk themselves into the grave before I let them interfere."

Then he remembered that he had to think of Tara as well as himself.

He wondered what he could do and had found it hard to sleep.

Now the same problem was raising itself again.

As he walked up the steps to the Tower he

thought there must be somebody.

Perhaps another McCairn would stay in the Castle without being tiresome, as his Aunt and her son were.

He had taken stock of Alastair since he had arrived.

He knew now there was something about the young man that was not quite right.

He did not know what it was.

Perhaps it was the education he had received—perhaps the way he was cossetted by his Mother.

But he did not live up to his opinion of what a boy of that age should be like.

It was obvious that he was fascinated by Tara, which Talbot could understand.

When it came to sports, and, after all, he had lived in Scotland all his life, Alastair seemed to have little to say.

Talbot had done his best to be congenial.

"How many salmon have you caught so far this season?" he enquired.

"I do not know," Alastair answered.

"You must have some idea," Talbot argued. "I have actually never caught salmon, so I shall certainly fish carefully and be very proud of my progress, once I know what to do."

He had said this at luncheon, and Tara had joined in, saying:

"It is most important to have the best gillie on the whole river to teach you. Once you have learnt how to throw a line, you will find it easy and, as I have found, very exciting!"

"I forgot you had done some salmon fishing," Talbot remarked. "Are you a good fisherman?"

"Of course," Tara said. "How could I be anything else when I almost fished from my perambulator!"

They laughed at that, and Talbot went on:

"Then you will have to teach me."

He nearly added: "As you taught me the Reels."

Then he remembered that his Aunt and Alastair were listening.

Tara shook her head.

"No. My Father did not teach me because he said it was always a mistake not to have the greatest expert available. I am sure on this river there are men who have not only fished since they could first walk, but also knew every inch of the river itself, every nook and corner where a fish might be lying."

"Very well," Talbot said. "I will make enquiries, but I shall let none of you watch me until I am really proficient."

Alastair had not joined in the conversation.

Talbot thought it equally strange that he was not interested in the grouse.

"Have you had a good hatching?" he asked.

"I do not know," Alastair answered.

"But, surely, as you have a moor of your own, you are interested in how the birds are doing?" Talbot persisted.

"Of course he is interested!" Lady Heather said sharply before Alastair could reply. "But I think you should see the Game-Keepers and talk to them."

"I have already thought of that," Talbot answered. "They are all coming to see me to-morrow morning."

"In that case, there is no need to question us," Lady Heather said. "If you ask me, I think you should make some changes where the Keepers are concerned. I suspect two of them as being extremely lazy."

Once again Talbot thought she was interfering and he therefore changed the subject.

He had, up until then, had no chance of speaking to Alastair alone.

He thought when he got to the Tower he would find that it was nothing more urgent than a brick missing from the battlements.

Or perhaps the standard pole had broken.

He would tell Alastair that he wished to find out for himself what was needed at the Castle, and not have him or his Mother eternally pointing out that something was wrong.

The door out onto the Tower was ajar.

As he went out into the sunshine he thought for a moment that Alastair was not there.

As the centre of the Tower ended with the big standard pole, it sloped upwards from the very edge of the battlements.

It was therefore slippery to walk on.

Talbot paused and slipped his feet out of the brogue shoes he had brought in London.

They were slightly large for him anyway, and he knew it would be impossible to walk in them on the sloping roof.

He took several steps forward in his stockinged feet.

Suddenly Alastair appeared from behind the door and slammed it to.

"Oh, there you are, Alastair!" Talbot said. "What do you want to show me?"

As he spoke, he saw that Alastair was holding a sharp dirk in his hand.

He was also moving towards him in a menacing manner.

Talbot took a step sideways and realised that the sloping tiles were slippery.

But not only naturally, also because oil had been poured on them.

Alastair was moving slowly and carefully towards him.

"What is all this about, Alastair?" Talbot asked. "And why have you got a dirk in your hand?"

"You are going to die!" Alastair said in a strange voice. "Die so that I can become Chieftain."

"Do not talk nonsense . . ." Talbot began.

"My Mother says you have no right here," Alastair said.

He spoke in a sing-song voice, as if he were repeating what he had heard rather than expressing his own opinion.

"You die and the Castle is mine! All the Castle—mine!"

He was coming nearer, and Talbot took another step backwards.

It was difficult to keep his balance.

He was aware it would be easy, if Alastair struck him with the dirk, to fall over the battlements.

Then he knew without words that this was just what Alastair, and doubtless his Mother, had planned.

That was why oil had been put on the tiles.

When he fell to the ground dead, it would merely be assumed that his death was due to his ignorance of Scottish Castles.

Alastair was coming nearer.

There was nothing he could do but move away from him.

"Now, listen, Alastair," Talbot said, "this is ridiculous! You cannot kill me without there being a great many enquiries about it. Then you will be charged with murder!"

"You die! You die because you fall," Alastair said in the same strange voice he had used before.

Talbot looked into his eyes.

He knew that the reason he had thought Alastair odd and not completely normal was because he was mad.

Now there was an insane look about him.

He was moving as if he were compelled to do so by some force outside himself, not by his own volition.

"Alastair, listen to me," Talbot said again.

Even as he spoke, he knew that his words were having no effect on his Cousin.

Alastair was intent on only one thing—destroying him.

As Talbot moved farther away, still with difficulty, he wondered how Alastair was moving without slipping.

He then saw Alastair had special shoes on his feet which were not affected by oil.

He wondered wildly if he could move round the tower and reach the door before Alastair got to him.

It was, however, difficult to do anything quickly, and Alastair was drawing nearer.

Talbot wondered if anybody would hear him if he shouted.

Then he yelled as loudly as he could:

"Help! Help!"

Because they were so high up, his voice seemed to be carried away by the wind.

He doubted, even if there was anybody in the garden, whether they would be aware of what was happening.

Nor would they get to him in time.

"Help!" he cried again.

He thought despairingly that only God could help him now.

* * *

Tara ran up the last steps and opened the Tower door.

She was surprised that it should be firmly shut.

Then, as she pushed it open, she heard Talbot cry "Help!" and moved swiftly out into the sunshine.

She heard Talbot shout again.

She was just about to answer him, when she realised that he was crouched down.

Just in front Alastair had his back to her.

Then, as he moved, she saw the dirk glinting in the sunlight.

Incredibly, she realised what was happening.

It needed only two more steps for Alastair to reach Talbot.

She knew he intended to stab him.

In which case, as the battlements were low, he would fall over them and crash to his death in the Court-yard below.

It all passed through her mind with the swiftness of an arrow.

Then, as if somebody were telling her what to do, she raised her arm.

With all her strength she threw at Alastair's back the dirk she had taken off the wall.

It hit him squarely between the shoulders.

Because it was old and rusty, it did not pierce his body or even the tweed coat he wore.

It made him stagger.

He threw out his hands for support, and the dirk, as it fell to the ground, struck him on the foot.

He gave a scream of pain and lifted up his injured foot.

As he did so, he fell sideways.

One moment he was there, the next he had disappeared over the battlements.

It happened so quickly that Tara could hardly believe she was not dreaming.

She stood staring at the place where Alastair had vanished.

There was nothing to show what had occurred except his dirk lying on the tiles.

Talbot could not hurry, for his stockinged feet were covered in oil.

He had no intention of falling as he had seen his Cousin do.

Step by step he moved until he reached Tara.

She was standing just outside the door into the Tower.

He looked down at her, and she gave a little sob and whispered:

"H-he was . . . going to . . . k-kill you!"

"I know," Talbot said, "and you saved my life."

He saw how pale and frightened she was.

As he put his arms round her, she clung to him as if she were afraid he was not really there.

"It is all right," he said soothingly, "you saved me."

She looked up at him wildly.

"I . . . I killed him!" she murmured.

"It was very brave of you," Talbot said. "It was a question of him or me."

She did not seem to understand.

He realised how shocked she was and pulled her closer still.

"It is all over," he said.

She stared up at him, and he very gently kissed her lips.

For a moment she was too stunned to realise what was happening.

Then, as Talbot held her closer still, his lips became more possessive.

She felt as if the sunshine dazzled her eyes, and at the same time moved in her breast.

Alastair was dead, but Talbot was kissing her.

It was the most wonderful thing that had ever happened.

To Talbot, the last few minutes, when he had thought there was no escape from Alastair, had been sheer undiluted torture.

It had frightened him as he had never been frightened before.

His Cousin was mad.

At the same time, Alastair had the strength to use a weapon against which he had no defence.

There appeared to be no escape.

He was wondering frantically what he should do, when he saw Tara come out onto the Tower.

His first thought had been that Alastair must not injure her.

If he had been prepared to kill him, he might also be prepared to kill her.

For two seconds, he forgot his own peril in his desire to save Tara from being hurt in any way.

He knew then, although it was rather late in the day to be aware of it, that she meant more to him than anyone else.

She must not be involved in this.

He knew if he had called out to her to go away, she would obey him.

Even as the thought came into his mind, he saw her raise her arm.

She aimed something she held in her hand at Alastair.

Talbot saw Alastair stagger and scream.

Just as it had seemed unreal to Tara, so it did

to Talbot. As Alastair disappeared over the battlements, he vanished out of sight.

It was fantastic, incredible!

Even as Talbot moved carefully back towards Tara, he found it hard to realise what had just happened.

Now, as he held her in his arms and kissed her, he knew it was something he had wanted to do for a long time.

He had fought against it.

He had told himself as he had told Henry that she was merely a girl he had known since she was a child.

She was of no interest to him other than that she could help him.

Then, as he kissed her, and went on kissing her, he knew that, for the first time in his life, he was in love.

His whole being responded to her.

Not just his body, but his heart, and vaguely what he recognised as his soul.

He knew, too, it was what he had always missed with Isabel and the other women to whom he had made love.

As he was aware of the innocent sweetness and the purity of Tara's lips, he knew that was what he had missed and what he had wanted.

'You are mine!' he thought as he kissed her. 'Mine, and nobody shall ever take you from me.'

To Tara, the Heavens had opened and the wonder and glory of it came from the Divine.

She had never been kissed.

But she had thought it would be very wonderful if it was by somebody she loved.

She knew now that what she had been feeling for Talbot was love.

She had, however, been too shy to admit it to herself.

He was not only the most handsome man she had ever seen, but quite the most interesting.

There was also something about him that told her he was exceptional, and that he had a great deal to give to the world.

She watched and listened to him.

It was almost as if somebody were telling her he had great potential and she must help him develop it.

When she was alone in bed the night before and thought about it, she laughed at herself for being so imaginative.

And yet the next day, when she saw him again, she knew that everything she felt about him was true.

She had to help him.

Somehow, by a miracle, he had brought her with him to the land to which she belonged, a land to which she knew he belonged too.

She had to make him understand, make him realise how much he could do for Scotland.

"He will never listen to me," she told herself despairingly.

And yet he had let her teach him the Scottish dances.

He had listened to everything she told him about

Scotland, and she felt she was becoming more and more useful.

It was a privilege that might have come from God.

Now he was kissing her, kissing her until she felt that nothing in the world existed except him!

They were floating in the sky, where no-one could hurt or harm them.

Talbot raised his head.

"My Darling, my sweet!" he said. "I love you! We will be married immediately, for I will never let you out of my sight."

For a moment, Tara felt as if she could hear the angels singing.

Then she murmured:

"Alastair . . ."

"I know," Talbot said, "and I suppose we will have to explain what happened."

"There be nae need tae do that, M'Lord!" a voice said behind them.

They both turned to look with astonishment at Ross, who was standing in the doorway.

"Ah saw what occurred, M'Lorrd," Ross said "an' Ah think it'd be better if naebody knows th' truth."

"What do you mean?" Talbot asked.

"Mr. Alastair were mad," Ross answered. "We all o' us ken that, an' he's been the same at the beginning o' every moon since he were a wee laddie."

"I find it hard to understand why I was not told," Talbot said.

Ross glanced over his shoulder as if he were afraid somebody might be listening.

Then he said in a low voice:

"Her Ladyship, who many in the Clan thinks is a Witch, has said that if anybody spoke o' it she'd curse them and th' curse'd follow them to th' grave and remain wi' their descendents in every generation that followed."

Both Talbot and Tara stared at him.

"Is that really true?" Talbot asked.

Ross nodded.

"Mr. Alastair be always kept at Her Ladyship's side an' out o' sight when th' moon be full."

"To-day he was following his Mother's instructions," Talbot remarked.

"She be determin'd to be rid o' ye, M'Lorrd," Ross agreed, "so that her son could be th' new Chieftain."

"It was she who drugged the haggis," Tara interposed. "That is why I followed you. The dogs ate it and both fell asleep."

There was no need for further explanation.

Talbot knew that if he had eaten only a little of the haggis he would have been bemused and sleepy.

It would then have been easy for Alastair to frighten him into falling over the battlements.

There was silence, until Talbot said:

"Now I know I am in Scotland! But you say no one must know, Ross. How can we manage that?"

"A scandal would be bad fur th' Clan, M'Lorrd, verry bad!" Ross said. "So when Her Ladyship's man-servant told ye tae come up here, ye found to your surprise that there be naybody here. If ye'll hand me th' two dirrks, Ah'll put them awa' so there'll be nae signs o' Mister Alastair. When ye come doon th' stairs, ye can say ye thought 't was a joke."

"I understand exactly what you are saying," Talbot said, "and thank you, Ross, for thinking of it."

He moved past Talbot, and picked up the two dirks that were lying almost side-by-side.

He then cautiously moved back to the door.

"Ah think, M'Lorrd," he said respectfully, "as Miss MacDowall has joined ye, ye should stay here awhile, enjoying th' view. Ah'll see tae everything. Ah'll say what has happened, and when Yer Lorrdship learns of it, ye'll be vastly surprised at th' tragedy which occurred when Mr. Alastair fell frae th' roof."

"Thank you, Ross," Talbot said.

The old man went from the Tower, shutting the door behind him.

Talbot pulled Tara against him.

"He is right," he said, "and it would do no good to let the Clan know that Alastair wanted to kill me."

"Suppose . . . he . . . had?" Tara asked in a frightened voice.

"It is something we both have to forget," Talbot answered, "and all we have to think about is that I love you, and you have to look after me."

"You know I . . . will do . . . that," Tara whispered. "But you must be very . . . very careful of . . . yourself."

Talbot laughed.

"I will be, because you have so much to teach me."

He kissed her gently before he added:

"And I have a great deal, my Lovely one, to teach you—about Love."

## *chapter seven*

THEY sat in the sunshine.

Talbot was kissing Tara until she could think of nothing but him.

There were no difficulties or troubles in the world.

At last he said:

"I suppose, my Darling, we ought to go down and see what is happening."

"I want to stay here for ever and ever," Tara said, "just with you."

Talbot smiled.

"It is what I would like, too, although in perhaps more comfortable surroundings."

"Anywhere would be . . . comfortable if . . . we were . . . together," Tara said.

"That is what we are going to be," Talbot answered, "and whatever anybody says, I intend to marry you as quickly as possible. Then you will be mine."

He kissed her again.

Her head fell back against his shoulder, and she shut her eyes.

The whole world had changed in these few minutes.

All she could think of was how much she loved Talbot, and how wonderful he was.

Reluctantly, knowing that time was passing, he got to his feet.

He put on the brogue shoes he had worn when he came up to the Tower.

He then opened the door.

As he did so, he took one glance at the oily surface of the tiles, which Alastair had set as a trap for him.

He thought that only God could have sent Tara to save him at the last minute from what would have been an ignominious and horrible death.

He walked to the top of the steps which led down to the corridor.

Then, turning round, he reached out to help Tara down.

He knew that because he was touching her it gave her a little thrill.

"Could anybody be more adorable?" he asked himself.

They moved slowly along the passage, and down the next flight of stairs.

Finally, they reached the First Floor.

Talbot was not surprised to see Ross waiting for them there.

He came towards them.

Talbot was aware that there were two footmen in the background.

"Ah regret tae tell Your Lorrdship," Ross said, "Ah have tragic news."

"What can that be?" Talbot asked in feigned surprise.

"It appears, My Lord, that Mr. Alastair fell from th' North Tower some time after breakfast. He must hae slipped, for he was found in th' Court-yard injured an', of course, nae langer breathin'."

"I can hardly believe it!" Talbot exclaimed. "Miss MacDowall and I have been up in the Tower, but there was nobody there."

"Ye must hae reached it, My Lorrd, after Mr. Alastair had fallen doon," Ross said. "Ah hae arranged for th' body tae be carried first tae th' Doctorr, then on to the wee Kirk up the Strath, 'til the Funeral takes place."

Talbot drew in his breath.

It was a relief to know that Alastair would not lie in the Castle.

"Mr. Alastair'll be buried next tae his Faither," Ross continued. "Her Ladyship has left in another carriage tae mak' all th' arrangements."

"I am sorry that I cannot personally commiserate with Her Ladyship over the tragic loss of her only child. She must be very upset."

"Her Ladyship seemed stunned when Ah gave her th' news," Ross said, "but, as Your Lorrdship'll ken, nothing could be done. The Tower be verry high, an' no-one could fall fra' it wi'out being killed instantly on the hard surface o' th' Court-yard below."

"I understand that," Talbot said. "Thank you, Ross, for arranging everything in my absence. I am only sorry I could not have been of assistance."

In a different tone of voice Ross said:

"Your Lorrdship will remember ye asked th' Elders tae come here this morn. They're waiting noo for ye in the Chieftain's Room."

Talbot looked at the Grandfather clock ticking away on the landing.

"Is it so late?" he asked. "I am afraid I had for-gotten the time. Of course I will go to the Elders immediately, but first I wish to have a word with Miss MacDowall."

Ross opened the door of the Drawing-Room.

They went inside, and when they were alone Talbot said:

"Wait here for me, my Precious. I have already planned what I want to say to the Elders. I will come back to you in what, I think, should be only a few minutes."

"What are . . . you going to . . . say?" Tara asked.

"I will tell you that when I return," Talbot answered. "Do not worry. I feel that we have been blessed as few people are fortunate to be, and now that Alastair is no longer here to menace my position, everything will be very much easier."

"I hope so . . . I do hope . . . so," Tara murmured, "and remember, the Elders are very important, at least . . . they think . . . they are."

"I remember everything you have ever told me," Talbot answered.

*142*

He kissed her gently and went from the Drawing-Room.

He knew without her telling him that while he was away, she would be praying for him.

He thought no man could be more fortunate than he was.

How could he have imagined anything like this a fortnight ago?

He was a man with no prospects, no money, and no hope of earning any.

Yet now he found himself a Chieftain and owner of a Castle.

And—more important than anything else—very much in love.

As he thought of Tara, he knew that all the other women in his life had faded away like pale ghosts.

He could hardly remember them because they were no longer of any importance.

He had the one woman who had always been in a shrine in his heart, although he had not been aware of it.

He reached the Chieftain's Room, and found a footman waiting to open the door for him.

He straightened his shoulders, and raised his chin.

He went into the room slowly.

The Elders were all seated.

The horned chair of the Chieftain was in front of them, waiting to be occupied by him.

"Good-morning, Gentlemen!" Talbot said.

They started to get to their feet, but he added:

"Please, do not rise. I must apologise for being late, but I was looking at the view from the top of the Castle. I was so entranced by the beauty of it all that I am afraid I lost track of the time."

He saw a smile on the elderly faces, as if they were pleased that that was the reason for his being delayed.

He went towards the Chieftain's chair, but he did not sit down.

Instead, he stood facing them and said:

"I have something to tell you, and I must ask for your understanding and your help. It is something I need desperately, and I am turning to you because I feel in your wisdom you will give me the answer I need."

It was Andrew who replied for the others, saying:

"Of courrse, M'Lorrd, we'll help ye, if it's possible."

Talbot smiled at him.

"You have been such a help already," he said, "that I feel that you and the other Elders will not fail me now."

"What is it ye want?" Andrew asked. "And perhaps, M'Lorrd, we should start by offering our commiserations on the death of Yer Lorrdship's Cousin, Mr. Alastair."

The way Andrew spoke made Talbot aware that he was not in the least upset by Alastair's death.

He thought, too, he could see an expression of relief on the faces of the other Elders.

"It was a terrible thing to happen to my Cousin,"

Talbot said, "and we must all send our condolences to my Aunt, Lady Heather, at the loss of her only child."

The Elders nodded their heads, and Talbot went on:

"My Cousin's death also affects me in a way I did not expect, and is the cause of my problem."

He knew, as he spoke, that everybody was listening to him intently.

Several of the Elders had their hands cupped to their ears so as not to miss anything he said.

"My problem is that Miss Tara MacDowall has consented to become my wife, and I wish to marry her at once," Talbot said quietly. "You can see that it makes it difficult for her to stay here without a chaperon in such circumstances. The Funeral will also mean that I, and the other members of the McCairns, will be in mourning for a month or so."

He paused, then was aware by the smile on Andrew's face how delighted he was by the news that he was to marry Tara.

He went on:

"What I am asking you, and of course I would wish nothing that would in any way hurt or damage the Clan, is whether it is possible for me to marry Miss MacDowall before the Funeral, and in fact before my relations are aware that Cousin Alastair is dead?"

He did not wait for the Elders to speak, but merely said:

"What I am going to do now is to leave you to think this over amongst yourselves. Please decide what you think is the right thing for me to do, how it affects the Clan and my position as Chieftain. I will, therefore, withdraw to another room and return in five minutes to learn of your decision, which, of course, I will abide by."

As he spoke he walked from the room.

He was aware that the Elders were surprised, in fact, astonished that he was leaving them to make so important a decision on their own.

He was sure that Andrew, if no-one else, would be on his side.

He went back into the Sitting-Room.

As the door shut behind him Tara turned from the window and ran across the room to throw herself into his arms.

"What is . . . happening? What . . . did they . . . say? Why are . . . you back so . . . quickly?"

Talbot did not answer, he merely kissed her.

She surrendered herself to the insistence of his lips.

When he knew she was no longer so tense, he raised his head.

"I will tell you exactly what I have done, my Darling," he said, "and I am sure you will approve."

They sat down on the window-seat in the sunshine and he related every word he had said.

"Oh, Talbot, that was clever of you!" Tara exclaimed. "They will be so thrilled that you have asked their advice, that I am sure they will agree we should be married before the Funeral takes place."

"That is what I thought," Talbot answered. "I

146

have also remembered that we must send the grooms to tell everybody who is coming to dinner to-night of Alastair's death. Will you arrange that with Ross? I imagine he must have a list of who has been invited. I must now return to the Elders."

"Yes, of course I will," Tara answered. "I am praying their answer will be the one we . . . want."

"My instinct tells me that my luck changed as soon as two people came into my life," Talbot said. "First Andrew, then you!"

"How could I have guessed," Tara said in a low voice, "that when you came looking for Papa and I opened the door to the most handsome man I had ever seen, that . . . you would . . . love me?"

"How could I do anything else," Talbot answered, "when you are not only the most beautiful person in all the world, but also good, and exactly what I need."

"I hope you will continue to think so after we are . . . married," Tara said.

"You can be certain of it," Talbot answered.

He kissed her passionately, because there were only two minutes left before he should return to the Elders.

He went back down the corridor.

As he did so, he prayed as he had not prayed since he was a small boy that they would give him the decision he wanted.

He went into the Chieftain's Room, and this time seated himself in the horned chair.

"Well, Gentlemen?" he asked.

Andrew, who had obviously been elected their

spokesman, rose to his feet.

"We have come to a decision, My Lord, which Ah hope will please ye."

"I hope so too," Talbot murmured.

"We, the Elders, think it will be some time before the Clan, except for those actually living in and around the Castle, will learn of Mister Alastair's death. Therefore we think it best and wisest for Your Lordship to be married late this evening in the Kirk, with as few people there as possible."

Talbot felt the relief sweep over him, but he did not speak, and Andrew went on:

"To-morrow we will inform the Clan in the village and the out-lying parts of the Estate that your Cousin, Mr. Alastair McCairn, has died in an unfortunate accident. There will be no mention of the marriage until after the Funeral."

"I can only thank you," Talbot said in a low voice.

"We also think it wise, if Your Lordship will agree," Andrew went on, "that your Grandfather's yacht—which at the moment is ready for service—should be used, if Your Lordship is considering a honeymoon."

He paused then went on:

"The *Sea Lion* can tak' ye to the Orkney Isles, or anywhere else ye fancy. That will mak' it easier when ye return for us to arrange the celebrations. The Clan will accept them with joy without being over-shadowed in any way by the Funeral, which'll be almost forgotten by then."

Andrew then sat down, saying:

"I hope, Your Lordship, that what we have suggested meets wi' your approval."

Talbot rose.

"Gentlemen," he said, "I was sure you would help me, and I can only thank you from the bottom of my heart for your kindness and understanding. I am delighted at the idea of being married this evening to Miss MacDowall, and I can only hope it will be possible for all twelve of you to be present as witnesses to our marriage in the Kirk. I will then, as you suggest, leave as soon as the Funeral is over, in my Grandfather's yacht. When my wife and I have been away for over a month, we will return and celebrate our marriage in the appropriate way with, of course, a feast. What I think the Clan would also enjoy is if it were combined with the Games, which, I am told, take place around that time of the year."

There was a general murmur of approval, and Talbot went on:

"It may seem, Gentlemen, a little strange when we are shadowed by the death of a McCairn, however, I would ask you to drink to my happiness."

There appeared to be no objection to this, and Talbot rang the bell.

When Ross appeared, he knew what was expected.

Talbot had no sooner given the order than a footman came in carrying a decanter of whisky on a tray.

Then he offered it to the Elders, who filled their glasses.

When the servants had withdrawn, they lifted them, saying in Gaelic:

"Good health to the Chieftain! May he be our guide and leader for many years to come!"

Talbot thanked them, and said to Andrew:

"May I leave it to you to contact the Minister, swear him to secrecy, and make all the arrangements for the decoration of the Kirk? I want my wife to remember this day as being one of happiness for us both."

"Ah'll see tae it, My Lord," Andrew agreed.

Talbot walked towards the door.

"I am going now to fetch Miss MacDowall," he said, "because I know she will want to thank you herself for your great kindness towards us."

He hurried down the corridor, burst into the room, and took Tara in his arms.

"They have agreed! We have won!" he said triumphantly. "We are being married secretly this evening. Then I am taking you away on a voyage on my Grandfather's yacht, which I did not even know I possessed!"

He kissed her before he said:

"It will be a voyage of discovery for us both, my Darling, and very, very exciting!"

He saw the tears of relief in her eyes, and kissed them away before he said:

"Now you must come and meet the Elders. You will want to thank them, and I know they will be delighted that I have chosen a real 'Scots Lassie' for my bride."

"That is true," Tara laughed. "Oh, Talbot, I am so happy!"

They went to the Chieftain's Room hand-in-hand.

As the Elders rose to their feet, Talbot knew from the way they looked at Tara that they admired her.

They also approved whole-heartedly of their Chieftain's choice of a bride.

* * *

Four weeks later, Talbot and Tara lay in the Master Cabin of the *Sea Lion*.

The sunshine was coming through the side of the curtains, which covered the port-holes.

Talbot reached out and drew his wife into his arms.

"I suppose, my Precious One, we should begin to think of going home."

"How shall we let them know when we will be there?" Tara asked.

"The Captain can send a message for us," Talbot replied, "and when we arrive at the Castle everyone will be waiting to celebrate our marriage."

Tara moved a little closer to him.

"Oh, Darling, it is so wonderful being here alone with you that I . . . dread going back to . . . the world . . . again."

"Whenever we wish to escape we will do so in this funny old vessel," Talbot said, "or perhaps a more up-to-date version of it, and visit the islands where the people have been so kind to us."

"It has been a wonderful . . . wonderful Honeymoon," Talbot said.

"That is what I have found," Talbot answered. "I do not believe anyone could be so soft, sweet, and perfect."

"Oh, Talbot, I hope you will always think that," Tara said. "I was so . . . afraid you might be . . . disappointed and find me . . . dull after all those . . . exciting . . . elegant women you knew in . . . London."

"I find everything about you irresistible," Talbot said. "And what do you know about 'elegant exciting women'? I have never talked to you about them."

"You underestimate your importance," Tara said. "I remember hearing my Father and Mother talking about you when you first left Oxford, and saying how women threw themselves into your arms even before you knew their names!"

Talbot laughed.

"I have never heard such nonsense! And if they did exist, then I have forgotten about them. All I can think of is an adorable 'Scots Lassie' who has captured my heart, and is going to make me the most important Chieftain in the whole of Scotland."

"Of course you will be that," Tara said. "You will have to go sometimes to Edinburgh so that you can speak to the politicians there, who are not making a strong enough appeal for Scotland in Westminster."

Talbot put his head back on the pillow.

He thought that during the past weeks he had not given a thought to London.

He had even forgotten Henry, his other friends, and everything he did there.

It was Tara who made him feel that, having married her, he possessed the most important thing in life.

Also, he undoubtedly belonged to Scotland.

As they had steamed from Island to Island in the Shetlands, he knew his heart beat faster at the beauty he saw everywhere.

He also thrilled to the first note of the pipes.

It was music which aroused in him feelings he had never known he possessed—pride and patriotism.

He felt it stir the part of his blood that was Scottish.

Tara had always believed it was stronger than the English half of him.

It was hard for him to put into words.

But he knew he would be prepared to die for Scotland.

While he lived, he would fight both physically and spiritually for the country to which he belonged.

Now, as he held Tara in his arms, he said:

"I love you! Are there no better words with which to express my love?"

"That is all I want to hear," Tara said "and, Darling, I love you. You are clever. You must make the Castle a meeting place for all the people who think like us—that Scotland must play a bigger and greater part in the British Isles than it does at the moment."

"We will do that," Talbot agreed.

Tara moved a little nearer to him.

"And also, my magnificent husband, it will be a home filled with love, not only for the Clan, but . . . also for our . . . children."

She whispered the last word, and Talbot's arms tightened.

"Do you think . . . ?" he asked after a moment's pause.

Tara lifted her face to his.

"I think I am . . . having . . . a baby. I am praying it will be . . . a son, as strong, brave, tender, and kind as you. He will carry on the crusade that you are going to lead, and in which I know you will be triumphantly . . . successful."

Talbot drew in his breath.

"A son, my Wonderful One!" he said. "Could anything be more perfect? And there is plenty of room for any number of children in the Castle!"

Tara gave a little laugh.

"One at a time!" she said. "But you are . . . pleased?"

"Pleased, ecstatic, delighted, and excited!" Talbot answered.

His breast was against her as he said:

"How can I ever thank God for giving you to me or be grateful enough that you came into my life just when I needed you?"

"I think our Fate was planned for us from the very moment we were born," Tara answered. "I feel sure that Papa, and, of course, your Mother, have been guiding us, until together with our children we will work for the land we love and which can contribute so much to the . . . whole world."

Because Talbot was deeply moved, he did not know what to say.

He could only kiss Tara.

At first reverently, as if she were infinitely precious and sacred.

Then, as the ecstasy of their kisses aroused within them a warmth like the sunshine, they were swept into the burning heart of the Sun itself.

As Talbot made Tara his, she knew they were in a Heaven of their own, where the pipes were playing.

## ABOUT THE AUTHOR

**Barbara Cartland**, the world's most famous romantic novelist, who is also an historian, playwright, lecturer, political speaker and television personality, has now written over 580 books and sold over six hundred and twenty million copies all over the world.

She has also had many historical works published and has written four autobiographies as well as the biographies of her mother and that of her brother, Ronald Cartland, who was the first Member of Parliament to be killed in the last war. This book has a preface by Sir Winston Churchill and has just been republished with an introduction by Sir Arthur Bryant.

*Love at the Helm*, a novel written with the help and inspiration of the late Earl Mountbatten of Burma, Great Uncle of His Royal Highness, The Prince of Wales, is being sold for the Mountbatten Memorial Trust.

She has broken the world record for the last sixteen years by writing an average of twenty-three books a year. In the *Guinness Book of World Records* she is listed as the world's top-selling author.

Miss Cartland in 1987 sang an Album of Love Songs with the Royal Philharmonic Orchestra.

In private life Barbara Cartland, who is a Dame of the Order of St. John of Jerusalem, Chairman of the St. John Council in Hertfordshire and Deputy President of the St. John Ambulance Brigade, has fought for better conditions and salaries for Midwives and Nurses.

She championed the cause for the Elderly in 1956, invoking a Government Enquiry into the "Housing Condition of Old People."

In 1962 she had the Law of England changed so that Local Authorities had to provide camps for their own Gypsies. This has meant that since then thousands and thousands of Gypsy children have been able to go to School, which they had never been able to do in the past, as their caravans were moved every twenty-four hours by the Police.

There are now fourteen camps in Hertfordshire and Barbara Cartland has her own Romany Gypsy Camp called Barbaraville by the Gypsies.

Her designs "Decorating with Love" are being sold all over the U.S.A. and the National Home Fashions League made her, in 1981, "Woman of Achievement."

She is unique in that she was one and two in the

Dalton list of Best Sellers, and one week had four books in the top twenty.

Barbara Cartland's book *Getting Older, Growing Younger* has been published in Great Britain and the U.S.A. and her fifth cookery book, *The Romance of Food*, is now being used by the House of Commons.

In 1984 she received at Kennedy Airport America's Bishop Wright Air Industry Award for her contribution to the development of aviation. In 1931 she and two R.A.F. Officers thought of, and carried, the first aeroplane-towed glider airmail.

During the War she was Chief Lady Welfare Officer in Bedfordshire, looking after 20,000 Servicemen and -women. She thought of having a pool of Wedding Dresses at the War Office so a Service Bride could hire a gown for the day.

She bought 1,000 gowns without coupons for the A.T.S., the W.A.A.F.'s and the W.R.E.N.S. In 1945 Barbara Cartland received the Certificate of Merit from Eastern Command.

In 1964 Barbara Cartland founded the National Association for Health of which she is the President, as a front for all the Health Stores and for any product made as alternative medicine.

This is now a £65 million turnover a year, with one-third going in export.

In January 1968 she received *La Médeille de Vermeil de la Ville de Paris*. This is the highest award to be given in France by the City of Paris. She has sold 30 million books in France.

In March 1988 Barbara Cartland was asked by

the Indian Government to open their Health Resort outside Delhi. This is almost the largest Health Resort in the world.

Barbara Cartland was received with great enthusiasm by her fans, who feted her at a reception in the City, and she received the gift of an embossed plate from the Government.

Barbara Cartland was made a Dame of the Order of the British Empire in the 1991 New Year's Honours List by Her Majesty, The Queen, for her contribution to Literature and also for her years of work for the community.

Dame Barbara has now written the greatest number of books by a British author, passing the 564 books written by John Creasey.

# AWARDS

1945    Received Certificate of Merit, Eastern Command, for being Welfare Officer to 5,000 troops in Bedfordshire.

1953    Made a Commander of the Order of St. John of Jerusalem. Invested by H.R.H. The Duke of Gloucester at Buckingham Palace.

1972    Invested as Dame of Grace of the Order of St. John in London by The Lord Prior, Lord Cacia.

1981    Received "Achiever of the Year" from the National Home Furnishing Association in Colorado Springs, U.S.A., for her designs for wallpaper and fabrics.

1984    Received Bishop Wright Air Industry Award at Kennedy Airport, for inventing the aeroplane-towed Glider.

1988    Received from Monsieur Chirac, The Prime Minister, The Gold Medal of the City of Paris, at the Hotel de la Ville, Paris, for selling 25 million books and giving a lot of employment.

1991    Invested as Dame of the Order of The British Empire, by H.M. The Queen at Buckingham Palace for her contribution to Literature.